I0731500

Russians and Rubles

A Helen and Frank Story

Thomas Morgan

TMH Publishing

Copyright © 2023 by Thomas Morgan

All rights reserved. No part of this publication may be reproduced, stored, or transmitted in any form or by any means, electronic, mechanical, photocopying, recording, scanning, or otherwise without written permission from the publisher. It is illegal to copy this book, post it to a website, or distribute it by any other means without permission.

This novel is entirely a work of fiction. The names, characters and incidents portrayed in it are the work of the author's imagination. Any resemblance to actual persons, living or dead, events or localities is entirely coincidental.

First edition

Cover Design: Jodi Parrish

ISBN (Print): 978-1-7376747-5-7

ISBN (ePub): 978-1-7376747-4-0

Also by Thomas Morgan:

*Helen and Frank: Getting Older and Finding Love with Food,
Wine, Theater, Music, Crime and COVID*

*Marinated Money: Love, Crime and Capers
in the time of COVID-19*

When the Lamb opened the second seal, I
heard the second living creature say, "Come!"
Then another horse came out, a fiery red one.
Its rider was given power to take peace from the
earth and to make people kill each other. To
him was given a large sword.

Revelation 6:3-4 (NIV)

Russians and Rubles

Introduction

The third installment of the *Helen and Frank* series takes our two stalwarts and their little band of conspirators through the tumultuous year of 2022. In two previous stories, Helen and Frank met in a memory care unit, and after a rocky beginning, fell in love, married, and grew wealthy during the plague of Covid-19. In *Russians and Rubles*, Helen's aggressive nature and Frank's money laundering skills attract attention from the wrong people. They tangle with an assorted group of miscreants, including American mobsters, Wagner Group operatives, shady bankers, and ambitious federal investigators.

A new plague arrived in 2022 amidst the disorder of Covid-19, crime, inflation, fentanyl overdoses, and a porous southern border. Vladimir Putin had his military invade Ukraine on February 28. He evidently expected what he called his special military operation to quickly overthrow the elected government in Kiev, allowing him to claim Ukraine as part of the Russian Federation. His mistake had deadly consequences. The world held its collective breath as the invasion unfolded, stalled, and settled into a European land war not seen in eighty years. Western countries rushed in equipment and materiel to help defend Ukraine. The most surprising finding from the war was the ineptitude and cruelty of the Russian military. Ukraine is a major supplier of grain to the world. The war of conquest by Russia brought death and fear of widespread famine. Plague, war, death, and famine never seem to leave us.

Frank and his nephew Vinnie jumped into the war on Ukraine with a plan to steal money from Russian oligarchs and send it to rebuild Ukraine. Helen and her friends joined the plan with enthusiasm and guile. Helen and Frank's rural location in St. Albans, Missouri, insulated them from urban chaos, but danger found them. Their involvement with criminal elements here and abroad compounded their peril. With wealth and influence, anyone can eventually overstep. It happened to Helen and Frank. They had to learn their lesson the hard way.

– Thomas Morgan

Chapter 1

December of 2021 brought no relief from Covid-19. The Omicron mutation of the virus, which had appeared around Thanksgiving, was highly infectious. It spread quickly, and efforts to contain it proved futile. Authorities argued about masks, vaccines, testing, isolation, and public gatherings. The one subject they dared not discuss was another lockdown. Various agencies issued conflicting guidelines and recommendations. When vaccinations were mandated for many private employees, the public was appalled by seeing healthcare workers, who had labored so hard and risked so much earlier in the pandemic, lose their jobs for refusing the vaccine. The irony was compounded when authorities recognized their mistake and issued exemptions to get essential people back to work. Even the definition of 'essential' was intensely debated. Test kits to detect infection were in short supply as were monoclonal antibodies to treat severe infections. Media personalities and pundits ignored the evidence that Omicron infection usually resulted in mild illness and that this variant might signal transition of the virus from pandemic to endemic status. The growing number of infected people disrupted travel and holiday activities. Health officials warned that hospitals could be overwhelmed. Rates of violent crime, suicide, drug overdoses and traffic fatalities increased. Despite this turmoil, people seemed determined to get on with their lives and mostly ignored everything that didn't affect their immediate needs.

At home in St. Albans, Missouri, on New Year's Eve, Francis Cabrini Palermo showered quickly and shivered as he toweled off. His bathroom was warm but the frigid cold outside seemed to permeate the entire house. He put on shorts and socks and inspected himself in the dressing room mirror. His fallen chest and protuberant belly were disappointing. He leaned forward for a closer inspection of his face and found it sagging too. Wrinkles and skin folds were winning everywhere he looked; his chest and legs seemed to be migrating to his stomach and hips. Even taking a deep breath and sucking in his abdomen failed to help. Frank thought he was beginning to look like a pear standing on toothpicks. He yawned and sighed. Based on what he saw, the year 2022 did not look promising for his body. Frank hoped his mind would hold up better. He pulled out his tuxedo and made a new year's resolution to get rid of the full-length mirror in his dressing room.

Helen came to the door and smiled. She looked beautiful in her little black dress and diamond stud earrings—the diamond solitaire on her left hand and a large blue sapphire rimmed by pave diamonds on her right hand—ready for cocktails with Barney and Moselle and the party to follow at the country club. "Admiring ourselves in the mirror again, are we?"

Frank, still in socks and shorts, turned and tried to return her smile. "Not much left anymore to admire. I think I'll get rid of the mirror ... don't like what it's showing me."

"That's why I don't have any full-length mirrors in my dressing room. I concentrate on my face. I can cover up the rest."

"Every part of you looks great." Frank was careful to omit the word 'still' from his attempt to praise her. "The ring enhances your beautiful blue eyes. I'll be with you in a minute."

"Don't hurry, and you won't have to tussle with the tuxedo. The club has cancelled the party," she said.

"Oh, no. What's going on?"

"Several members of the band called in sick this afternoon, and the wait staff is short-handed because of Covid. The general manager texted his apologies for such short notice, but they simply can't pull it off. Covid is turning everything upside down again."

"I'm not surprised, my dear. I was beginning to wonder if any of the members would show up. Everybody's afraid of Covid again because of this variant. This damn virus is the curse that keeps on cursing, but we can still go have drinks with Barney and Moselle. We'll play some music and party with them."

"Afraid not, darling. Moselle just texted me too. She thinks she's coming down with something. She's afraid it might be Omicron, and she's been vaccinated."

"Can Barney come up here? I can ice a bottle of Champagne, and there's Prosecco in the wine cooler."

"Negative on that too. They're both self-isolating ... they don't want to spread anything until they know what's happening. I don't blame them. I think we should self-isolate too. We've been around them a lot in the last few days. It looks like we're on our own tonight."

Helen and Frank's New Year's Eve of 2021 had begun with big plans, but it ended with a half-bottle of Prosecco and the rerun of a musical program on PBS. They were in bed by eleven p.m. with the shared hope that 2022 would be a better year.

∽

New Year's Day dawned cold and cloudy. The distant Missouri River far below them looked like a giant gray snake. They had lox and bagels with the usual trimmings and finished the Prosecco, which had gone flat. Vincenzo Alessandro Palermo, Frank's nephew, called at eleven a. m. from Chicago. Frank put him on speaker phone.

"Happy New Year, you two. I'm guessing you partied all night and are just waking up."

"Our entire evening crashed and burned. I'm afraid Covid won again," Frank said. "We stayed home and watched television."

"Same here. Chicago is trying to lock down again ... at least that's what the schoolteachers are saying. I think we'll be working from home for a while in the waste management operation ... except for the collection teams. They'll be out there making a few pick-ups, but that'll be it."

Frank paused. He sensed Vinnie wanted something from them but was having trouble getting to the point. "How's business, Vinnie? I imagine the East Coast people are pretty much running waste management by now."

"Right. I'm almost back fulltime with the commercial real estate business and the transition plans you put in." Vinnie took a deep breath. "Say ... Frank. I've been trying to find Rachel Bruggemann, but I'm coming up empty. Can you help me?"

Helen jumped in. "Vinnie, I think you're interested in her. You want to date her, am I right?"

Vinnie hesitated again. "She's very attractive ... and smart. I'd like to get to know her better."

Now Frank hesitated. "Here's the deal, Vinnie. Rachel got very anxious about Tony Ragusa and the SPAC deal that went bad, and I think she was right to be anxious. We were dealing with some very unsavory people at the time. She requested that we arrange for her to disappear ... at least for a while, and we helped her. I'm glad you're having trouble finding her."

"I understand. Maybe you could contact her ... see if she wants to talk to me. It wouldn't be about business. It would be a purely social contact."

"Vinnie, I'll talk to her, but I think this is a bad idea. If you start seeing her, your colleagues in New York and South Florida are bound to find out, and Vito and Patsy may think they still have a score to settle with her."

Helen nodded in silent agreement.

"They're not my colleagues! I keep them at arms-length. They're pretty much running waste management up here now after I helped them get started. I'm just barely involved with them anymore. I kept my end of the bargain. Now I want to be done with the whole lot of them."

Frank was not convinced. "Alright, Vinnie, I'll contact her and see if she wants to hear from you. Please stop trying to find her while I do this. I'll get back to you, Okay?"

When Frank put down the phone, Helen said, "I think you'd be making a big mistake if you pull Rachel back into this. She could get hurt."

"I want to have some control if they start seeing each other. If I don't contact her, he'll find her anyway. You remember how he always found us when we tried to hide. And I'll bet his East Coast friends will find her through him."

"You'd better warn her about this."

"She's all grown up. She knows about Vinnie and those people. She can make her own decisions, but I'd like to know what she's doing. I almost feel like she's our daughter."

Helen frowned and shook her head in disbelief. Frank left an encrypted message for Rachel through a confidential server. He told her that Vinnie wanted to see her socially and asked her to get back to him with her decision. When he didn't get a response for several days, he began making plans to drive to Florida where he would stay at his lakefront cabin for two months. Helen had decided not to accompany him. She told him the little cabin in Interlachen was too rustic for her. She did insist that Barney accompany him on the trip down and then fly back from Jacksonville. Frank was packing when he began to notice a headache and sore throat coming on. Then fever increased, and every part of his body began to ache. He took an Advil that gave little relief. By the next day, the malady had spread into his chest with congestion and a cough.

The day before he was scheduled to leave, Helen said, "I've seen you popping my Advil. Are you okay?"

"I think it's just a little head cold, but it seems to be getting into my chest and the rest of my body."

"You probably have Omicron. I have a home test kit. Let's check you out."

Frank reluctantly agreed. He had never been fond of doctors and nurses, particularly when they began ordering tests and telling him what to do. He had also heard that the rapid antigen tests were little better than a coin-flip for Omicron. When the test registered negative, he felt relief and returned to packing. He and Barney would make the drive to Florida over two days. Frank would drop him off at the Jacksonville airport for his return flight before continuing to his lakefront cabin in Interlachen. He could already feel the warm sunshine. He had fond memories of the little cabin on beautiful Lake Susan.

The next morning, Helen said, "You don't look so good. You're pale. You look like what my mother used to call peaked. I have another test kit. Let's check you again. I hear sometimes the tests can be negative before they turn positive."

When the second test returned positive, Frank felt despondent, and Helen was vindicated. "See, I told you. You've got Covid. You need to call your doctor and get some medicine. Now you'll give it to me too."

"I think you gave it to me. You're the one who's always going down to the club and having lunch with Moselle. I stay up here on the bluff and don't see anybody. And I'm not calling my doctor. I'm just not that sick, and I know she'll say to stay home and do exactly what I'm doing."

"Whatever you say, Dr. Palermo. Anyway, I'm sleeping in the far bedroom and staying away from *you*."

Frank did call his doctor, who told him to stay home and keep taking Advil or Tylenol if he felt feverish. She also suggested he use an inhaled steroid for the cough. She called in a prescription for a budesonide inhaler, which he did not fill when he learned the cost. After several days of extreme fatigue and cough, he slowly began to regain some stamina. The cough lingered. He resisted any additional medication and by the third week of January felt sufficiently improved to depart for Florida. Helen said no to this idea, insisting that he remain at home for another week. She communicated this decision by cellphone from the other end of the house.

When Helen thought he was no longer infectious, she returned to his end of the house and began to ply him with canned chicken soup, vitamins, minerals and several herb mixtures. After three days of her ministrations, Frank was determined to depart no matter what his condition. He put his investments on hold, packed his car, picked up Barney, and they left for Florida on the first day of February.

❧

The trip to Florida was uneventful. Barney insisted on accompanying Frank to the lake cabin and helped him move in, which was fortuitous because the cabin and the rowboat needed some minor repairs. After a week when they had set everything to rights, Frank drove Barney to the Jacksonville airport for his return trip to St. Louis. Frank returned to the little cabin on Lake Susan and prepared for two months of peace and quiet. Helen had dispatched him to Florida with a supply of vitamins, minerals and herbs. She texted him daily to be sure he was taking care of himself, which meant that he was doing what she had instructed. Frank quickly found that he preferred the isolated cabin a year ago when he and Helen were hiding from Tony and had shut down all communication to the outside world. He texted Helen that he was trying to recapture that time by turning off his cellphone.

The Florida sunshine worked its magic. As Frank felt his strength return, the cough subsided. He had never lost his sense of taste or smell. By the middle of February, he was out in the rowboat daily, trying to outwit the fish, which seemed to have gotten smarter since last year. His solitude helped him realize that he missed Helen's wit and snappy repartee. He began having erotic dreams about her—dreams he had long ago decided he would never have again. Out in his boat, he could smell the sweet scent from early blooming grapefruit trees around the lake. He imagined he could smell Helen and feel her touch. She had become integral to his life.

He decided he would only stay one month in Florida. If she would not come to him, he would have to go to her.

He turned on his cellphone the last week in February to inform Helen of his decision and found a text message from Rachel. She simply wrote 'Thank you for getting me together with Vinnie. We've had two dates. I think he's fabulous.' There were two heart emojis at the beginning and end of the message. Helen had also texted him that Vinnie had found Rachel and was dating her. The remainder of his text messages were requests for donations.

Migratory waterfowl landing on the lake and departing on their way north cemented Frank's decision. He decided he would return to St. Louis at the end of February. If Rachel's new relationship with Vinnie became public knowledge, he wanted to try to exert some control. He texted Helen, shut down the cabin, drove to the Jacksonville airport and took a Southwest flight to St. Louis.

Helen met him at Lambert Airport. They kissed and walked directly to her Uber. Frank had only a small carry-on bag. His Florida clothing would be useless in St. Louis weather in March. "I'm glad to see you," he said. "I really missed you. The little cabin felt empty without you."

"You really came back to see about Rachel, didn't you?"

"I came back to see you, but I'm worried about her. I guess Vinnie found her. I was surprised at how quickly they got together."

"Prepare to be more surprised," she said. "They're in Vegas as we speak. I think they're getting married."

Chapter 2

War broke out in Europe on February 24 when Russia invaded Ukraine. This was not a small incursion. The Russian military clearly intended to roll over Ukraine in a few days and quickly install a more complaint government. The people of Ukraine did not cooperate with this plan. They bravely fought against the invaders. Elsewhere, politicians of every stripe postured and bloviated. After a few days, the implications of what Russia had done registered in Europe, and NATO members and neighboring countries began to pour defensive weapons and humanitarian aid into Ukraine.

Frank had been so isolated at Lake Susan that he did not know of the Russian buildup around Ukraine's borders. He had no television, and he had turned off his cell phone for two weeks. Everyone was talking about the war when he arrived at the Jacksonville airport. Cable news kept repeating the same clips of Russian tanks rumbling down boulevards. The same thing was happening at the St. Louis airport when he arrived home. Commentators breathlessly repeated that there had not been a military action of this magnitude in Europe since the end of World War II.

He mentioned the war to Helen as they walked to her Uber ride. "What do you think about Ukraine? Everybody's talking about it. Do you think they can hold out?"

"They've already held out longer than anyone thought. The talking heads on TV say they must have had more defensive weapons than anybody knew. The world has turned against Russia. Governments in Europe are rushing in defensive weapons in the last few days. This is getting ugly and fast. The people are all fighting ... I'm talking about civilians. You should see the TV coverage. They're shooting it out on the streets in the big cities ... probably in the whole country, but it's not on TV."

"I guess I missed it. Maybe I shouldn't have turned off my phone."

"The Russians have been building up their forces around Ukraine for over a month. Everyone expected this to happen. You'd better check with our investment people. The stock market is down, and the price of oil and gas is going up. Putin and his oligarchs must like that development."

"It makes me wonder why he did this ... invading a next-door neighbor. Is it about the real estate or is it part of an investment plan?"

"Why not both? He's a cold, calculating man. And he's smart. I'll bet he played these financial angles. He had to know what would happen with the markets when he started a land war in Europe."

"I'll check it out. Here I go away for a month, and the world goes haywire. Now, please tell me what you know about Vinnie and Rachel."

"First of all, I'm sorry to be the one to tell you, but the world doesn't revolve around you. As for the happy couple, I've already told you what I know. He found her in Omaha. They've been quietly dating. It's obviously gotten serious ... and quickly. Now they're in Vegas. I think they're getting married."

"How do you know about the marriage part?"

"Rachel hinted at it in her last text. She said she had found the right person and didn't see any reason to wait any longer.

Darling, beneath the façade of cool calculation, she strikes me as an impulsive young lady."

"Waiting longer for what? Are you talking about her biological clock? How old is she anyway?"

"I think she's thirty-seven. So, it is about her biological clock ... at least in part. But she seems genuinely crazy about him. I think he's smitten with her."

Frank grimaced. "When can we see them? Can we get them to come down here for a few days?"

"You should talk to him. He's still got the plane. Barney told me he cancelled the lease arrangement on it. I think it cost him a lot of money to do that. He's been really trying to impress her, and money doesn't seem to matter at this point."

"It's going to matter if he runs out of it. And a lot of what he's spending is our money right now. We're helping finance his shift into remote work."

On their late afternoon ride from the airport to their home in St. Albans, the browns and grays of a late Missouri winter seemed to close around Frank. It was entirely different from the bright blue of Lake Susan and the surrounding greenery of the pines and scrub bushes in Interlachen. Helen told him that the mask mandate in St. Louis County had been lifted the day before he arrived, but he could see some people wearing masks as they drove along. Their Uber driver was masked. He had not seen a mask on anyone during his time in Interlachen. Only when he arrived at the Jacksonville airport did he begin to see people wearing masks.

❧

After a few days at home, Frank began to reassume financial oversight of their investments. During his time in Florida, he had left their money in the control of several financial advisors at his bank. He was pleased to note that his investments in oil and gas had appreciated remarkably with the onset of war—one good outcome for him about this stupid war. As he checked the categories, he was surprised to find that twenty million dollars had been allocated to an outside investment firm identified only as First Baltic Bank. He looked up the bank on the internet and saw that it was based in Chisinau, Moldova, with a branch in Estonia. A Baltic bank in a land-locked country near the Black Sea seemed strange. He called one of his investment advisors at his bank.

"I'm inquiring about First Baltic Bank," Frank said to Dmitri Scull, one of his advisors. "I've been reviewing my summaries. I don't understand why you put our money with them."

"Yes, sir, Mr. Palermo," Scull said. "We put a small amount with them because of their performance with currency shifts in that region. They have an admirable record in predicting currency trends."

"Dmitri, I don't think this is the time to be putting money into that part of the world. There's a war going on over there."

"Yes, sir, that war has been an unpleasant surprise, but First Baltic has had your investment for about a month now while you were on vacation. Their annualized return is projected to be about twenty percent."

"With currency speculation, gains can become losses overnight. I'm sure you are aware of that. And I don't see the connection between Moldova and Estonia. Who's running the bank over there?"

"His name is Val Constantin. We've worked with him for over three years. His bank's earnings have been very satisfying for a few of our higher net worth clients."

"Val Constantin? I've never heard of him."

"Well ... he's heard of you, Mr. Palermo. He specifically asked to manage a portion of your portfolio. He calls you the maestro of marinated money although I'm not sure what he means by that. When I couldn't reach you during your vacation, I checked with your nephew in Chicago. Vincenzo has heard of Mr. Constantin, and he told me to go ahead with the transfer."

Frank was angry. "Dmitri, in the future when you need permission to move my investments around, check with my wife, not my nephew."

"Yes, sir. We'll certainly remember that in the future. Do you want me to get your money out of First Baltic?"

"Not yet. Let it ride until I can find out more about what's going on. I'll get back to you."

Frank put down his phone and looked at Helen. "Did the bank tell you they were putting our money into an outfit called First Baltic Bank?"

"No, darling. I haven't heard from them since you went to Florida."

"They're free-lancing with our money. We're lucky that damn bank only has a part of our portfolio. I need to talk to Vinnie. We have to get Barney in on this too. We need a brain trust. Somebody knows more about us than I would like. If we can pry the newly-weds apart long enough to talk to us, I want to do a video conference. Jesus, Mary, and Joseph, if I'm the maestro of marinated money, this guy Constantin sounds like he owns the orchestra and finances the whole operation."

The war in Ukraine raged on with reports of horrendous numbers of civilian casualties. Stock markets sagged, and the price of oil kept going up. The president of Russia, Vladimir Vladimirovich Putin, indirectly threatened nuclear war if anyone interfered with his plans to conquer Ukraine. As the Covid crisis seemed to be winding down, a huge humanitarian crisis had arisen--a crisis that featured actual existential questions. Would Putin unleash his nuclear arsenal over control of Ukraine? That question energized pundits and generated anxiety in half the population of the Western world, mostly those who could remember the Cuban Missile crisis. To add insult to injury, Putin offered to evacuate civilians in besieged Ukrainian cities to Russia.

Frank finally arranged his video conference with Vinnie, Rachel, Barney, and Helen attending. "Thanks for joining us," he said. "Are congratulations in order? Are you two married yet?"

Rachel laughed and raised her left hand to show a huge diamond on her ring finger. "Two days ago," she said, "at the little chapel around the corner."

"That's wonderful news," Helen said. "We want you two newlyweds to come see us when you get back. We'd like to give you a little party and introduce you to our friends. We're so happy for you."

Frank tried to smile. "Please accept my congratulations too. Now, I'm sorry to mix business with pleasure, but we've got a problem here, and I need your help. I think we're on a secure encrypted link here so I'm going to put it to you straight."

Smiling faces became somber. "Here's the deal," Frank said. "While I was in Florida an imbecile at my bank put a chunk of our money into an outfit called First Baltic Bank. It's in Moldova with a branch in Estonia. The picture is still murky at this point. As best we can find out, this bank is set up to launder money all over Eastern Europe. The branch in Estonia gives them EU credibility, and the outfit in Moldova sits in a grey political zone that allows them financial flexibility. They finance arms and drug sales, they're dealing in rare earth metals, and they're helping Russia sell its oil. They move money and crypto around to make all this happen, and they're pros at it." Frank took a breath. "Vinnie, my banker tells me you gave him the go-ahead to send them our money."

"That's right, Frank. When your investment guy called me and I couldn't get you, I checked with Patsy and Vito. They know the bank, and they said to do the deal."

"That's what I was afraid of, Vinnie. I think that bank's as crooked as your friends on the East Coast. Now I find out the head of First Baltic actually solicited our investment. He's calling me the maestro of marinated money. That means he's been listening in somehow on what we were doing with Tony's money. He knows way too much about us. I'll bet they could teach us a thing or two about money laundering. Here we are mixed up with these people, and a war's going on over there."

"My dear uncle, Vito and Patsy are not my friends, but they know things we don't. It sounds like we're going to need their help if this bank is as crooked as you say."

"Let's start with the five of us," Frank said. "Barney is collecting information on Constantin and his bank. Vinnie, I need you to find out more about what Vito and Patsy know about this bank. Helen and I will get more information on what the bank is doing with our money. Rachel, I'm hoping you will agree to probe the bank electronically. Their interior files would be very interesting."

"Whoa ... just a minute," said Rachel. "Here I am just married, and you're pulling me into another of your situations. I could have been killed the last time. I thought I had retired from this stuff."

Frank smiled. "I'm simply asking. It's not a command. I'm in no position to tell anybody what to do. But please think about it. I'm hoping we can reconvene on video in two days. I'm also hoping that all of you will come to a party we want to give for the newly-weds when you come back from Vegas."

***

By the first week of March, a worldwide crisis developed around the price of nickel—a metal essential for electric vehicle batteries and stainless steel. Russia was a big nickel producer, and a coming shortage was expected, although sanctions had not yet been applied to nickel. A big Chinese nickel producer had placed some forward bets on nickel prices. With nickel prices shooting up, the Chinese company, Tsingshan Group, could not cover its hedging bets, resulting in what financial people call a short squeeze. The London Metal Exchange shut down electronic trading in nickel for over a week to allow time to equilibrate price and supply. The exchange also cancelled some transactions that had occurred earlier in the day before the suspension of trading. Financial commentators predicted that rapidly increasing prices would extend to other commodities coming from Russia, such as zinc, caladium, and wheat. When the London metal market reopened to electronic trading on March 16th, the price of nickel dropped so quickly that the exchange shut down again. The price continued to fall over the next several days, forcing the market to shut down trading each day. Large banks that had financed the hedging bets continued to negotiate with Tsingshan to cover their losses. The London Metal Exchange was owned by a Hong Kong conglomerate, and financial experts said the metal exchange's irregular behavior was another example of the financial world's deference to China.

In Nassau, Bahamas, Pasquale Salerno and Vito Ragusa met at Sunshine Investment Bank for their quarterly review of financial activities. Patsy represented organized crime in South Florida, and Vito represented the Five Families in New York City.

Vito looked up from his summary sheets and said, "We're doing well with all the financial upheaval going on right now, but that little bank in Moldova is really doing good things with our money. Everything's paying off. I don't understand the nickel thing, but that short squeeze worked for us."

"The bank's returns are better than I expected. That must be why Vinnie Palermo keeps asking about it. I think his uncle Frank put some money with them too."

"If Frank put some money with First Baltic, we should get him and Vinnie together with Val," Vito said. "Val can tell them to cool it. We don't need any publicity about that bank. It's our private gold mine." Vito paused and looked up from his summary sheets. "You know those charitable contributions we got so much credit for a while back really came from Frank Palermo, don't you?"

"You sure about that? I thought you said you couldn't track where that money came from."

"We finally figured it out. Frank covered his trail pretty well. He's really good at hiding money. I think our guy Val at the bank wants to use him too. Old Frankie boy can wash money with the best of them."

Patsy frowned. "You're talking about two different things here. Frank can't pull his money out and start working with Val at the same time. Which way do you want it?"

"Let Val figure it out. He'll be in New York later this month. He only communicates with us in person and outdoors. He won't do it any other way. He's more worried about security than we are. We can have Vinnie and Frank sit down with him in a park up there. I still think we should get Frank to pull his money out of First Baltic. He's not one of us."

"What about the woman?" Patsy asked.

"You talking about Helen Palermo, old Frank's wife?"

"Yeah, she's the one. I hear she's trigger happy. She's always packing, but she'll have trouble doing it in New York. I don't think she'll be a problem if she tags along. Anyway, even if she's carrying, she's not going to shoot anybody in Central Park in broad daylight. Sammy Mancuso tells me she's okay as long as you don't make her mad."

"Let's go ahead and see if we can set up the meet in New York. Val probably won't fly to Missouri. He'll think that's beneath his dignity or something. He always wants people to come to him."

With that statement, the center of the Palermo family wealth had shifted from Chicago to St. Louis, at least in the minds of Pasquale Salerno and Vito Ragusa. They were not alone. Frank's financial successes were becoming known almost everywhere.

Chapter 3

Frank and Vinnie met Val Constantin at the south end of Central Park at ten a.m. on March 24. They found a dapper man sitting on a bench at the east end of the Pond. Their instructions said don't approach him; stand still and wait to be searched. Then follow him to another bench for the interview. They did as they were instructed. Two silent men with shaved heads and neck tattoos appeared, frisked and scanned them, and pointed them to follow Constantin.

The weather was ideal—no topcoats necessary—with flowering trees beginning to bud. A few aspiring birds sang. Constantin looked to be about fifty, dressed in a bespoke blue pin-striped English suit and cap-toe shoes, carrying an umbrella in his left hand. He even wore a black bowler hat--an appearance straight out of Agatha Christie in Frank's estimation. As the threesome approached a bench, Constantin motioned them to sit. He stood before them at a distance of about six feet.

"You're punctual, I like that," he said. "I am happy to meet you. I've heard impressive things about you, but please let me make my point. I would like to interview the elder Mr. Palermo on how he handles money."

Frank couldn't place the accent. It was definitely European, somewhere east of Germany, perhaps Russian. "I handle it the same way I'm sure you do—carefully."

"Yes, but you can make it shape-shift. You call it marinated money. I think of it as invisible money."

"I'm sure I'm not telling you anything new. You need a cooperative bank, which I understand you already have. You shift it between cash and crypto. You disperse it and reassemble it several times. Then you make it appear in Euros or dollars or whatever specie you prefer. Next you park it somewhere offshore until you need it. That's the short version."

As I suspected," Constantin said. "The only thing you've left out is an African connection. That's where you turn it into money that looks even more legitimate and hard to trace."

"We bow to you with respect," Frank said. "You're out of our league, but I'm not sure why we're here. Did you want to give us an award?"

"Your reward will be lucrative. I wish to employ you."

"You already have a chunk of my money. Was that the entrance fee? Now you want to put us on your payroll?"

"Think of it as more of a consulting arrangement, Mr. Palermo. We'll have a trial period with your money. After that, I will send you our money to be marinated, as you say. You do that and take a three percent management fee when you're done. Then you send it back to me."

Vinnie jumped in. "What you're talking about is a decision for Uncle Frank to make. I'm not sure where I fit in."

"You fit in because you have large cash flows in your construction and leasing accounts. "That is where the money goes in and where it comes back out after it's been put through your cleaning process."

Frank smiled. "Suppose we wanted to enter into this business arrangement with you, how would the money move between us?" He was intrigued by Constantin's audacity and savoir faire. He was also trying to sound experienced at this sort of thing.

"That part is simple. We would have a consulting arrangement. The money would come in small increments into an account I would set up for you at a bank in Limassol, Cyprus. Once you've processed it, you'd return it to the Limassol bank minus your consulting fee. Your three percent fee would be calculated on the amount you return."

Constantin waited and then said, "Please take your time. Think it over. Discuss it with your colleagues. In the meantime, I suggest you join me for lunch at Benoit. They keep a good midday table, and their wine cellar is adequate."

After a three-hour lunch of escargot, cassoulet, lamb loin, and fresh fruit with crème fraiche, all fueled by several bottles of 2009 Chateau Leoville Barton, Constantin had his driver take Frank and Vinnie to Teterboro Airport across the Hudson River in New Jersey, where Vinnie's plane awaited them. Their flight was delayed because Helen, Moselle and Rachel had been shopping in Manhattan with an emphasis on Fifth Avenue, with Barney along for security. The women arrived late with numerous packages and shopping bags...and fully animated about their purchases. Barney looked weary. The sextet finally departed for home two hours later than scheduled.

Once in the air they seemed to be chasing the setting sun westward. After the women had exhausted conversation about their shopping adventures, they wanted to hear about the mysterious Val Constantin, which led to the six of them taking seats in the dining area of the Gulfstream G280. The three women sat facing the men. Frank thought their arrangement looked like a looming verbal battle of the sexes. Barney immediately reclined his seat and fell asleep. Shopping tires men. It usually invigorates women.

"Please start with Constantin," Helen said. "What did you think of him? Did he give you back our money?"

"He was pretty much what I expected," said Vinnie. "Very polished and debonair. He was all business in the park. In the restaurant he was all about economics and the folly of war. He wouldn't talk business in the restaurant. It was hard to place his origin ... I'm thinking maybe Poland."

"There was something Swiss about him," Frank said, "with maybe a slice of Russian."

The three women laughed. "He sounds like a cipher already," Moselle said.

"What did he want?" asked Helen. "You two are being very sly about what you did today."

"We were waiting for an opportunity to speak, my dear. I'm glad you ladies had such a good time shopping. And you owe Barney a big debt of gratitude for putting up with you."

"What did he want?" asked Moselle and Rachel in unison.

"Well, first of all we had a good meal although it was a little heavy for lunch," Frank said.

The three women glared at him. Frank smiled and said, "The short version is Constantin wants us to help him wash money. He calls it invisible money. He thinks we're good at that sort of thing. If the deal works out, he will deposit twenty-five million dollars in a bank in Limassol, Cyprus. It's our money plus a little of his. It's clean money, but he wants to watch us launder it. If we pass the test, he'll start sending us what I assume is dirty money to clean."

"He wants you to launder our perfectly clean and legitimate money? I don't believe this." Helen frowned at Frank.

"I think it's how he checks out our performance and learns our secrets. He strikes me as a very calculating sort of guy."

"You can't be serious about doing this," Helen said. "This man is probably connected to every gangster in Eastern Europe."

"I'll bet you're right about that. But there was a whiff of desperation in what he was pitching us. He was trying too hard. I'd sure like to know who's got money in his bank." Frank looked at Rachel when he spoke.

"What would you do if you knew?" Rachel replied.

"If it's Putin's money or from his oligarchs, I think we should try to divert some of it to rebuild Ukraine."

Helen groaned and Rachel laughed. "I know where you're going with this," the younger woman said. "You want me to hack their accounts."

"If would all depend on what we find out. If we could take some money from that pack of Russian thieves and murderers, I would be a happy man. Their greed has made them insanely rich and just about ruined Russia."

"I'd have to use some of my resources in Southeast Asia. The Eastern European network is probably already working with this Constantin guy."

"Rachel, not you too!" Helen said. "These people are probably more dangerous than the mob here in the States."

"I'm just thinking about it." Rachel smiled, leaned back, and closed her eyes. A full day of shopping with Helen and Moselle had exhausted the new bride.

"I'm just thinking about it too," Frank said. "I guess I'll have to check with the Feds if we get into this deal with Constantin."

❧

The humanitarian crisis in Ukraine worsened. After three weeks of war, the Russian invaders appeared to be stalemated by the brave Ukrainians. Even retired U.S. generals on television were saying this was the case. The Russian forces were estimated to be taking thousands of casualties. In response, the Russian air force poured long-range bombs and cruise missiles into the cities, increasing urban destruction and civilian deaths. The new strategy clearly was intended to discourage Ukraine's defenders by flattening the cities. NATO members continued to send defensive weapons to Ukraine, but the alliance refused to commit troops or airpower.

Frank lay on the couch in his office and watched the carnage unfold on the cable news channels. He had been three days home from the New York trip, but he felt paralyzed and helpless by this war. He was playing Mozart's *Requiem* softly on the house stereo and drinking a 2007 Barolo when Helen came in, picked up the remote, turned off the television and took away his bottle of Barolo.

"That's enough," she said. "You've turned into a couch potato. And you're drinking too much. You need to move on. You can't do anything about the war."

"I know ... I know I'm vegetating, but this is the worst thing I've ever seen. I've sent relief money. I pray for peace every day, but I feel so helpless."

She leaned down and kissed his forehead. "Darling, I know this is upsetting you. We are all hoping for peace. It's upsetting everyone, but you're letting it keep you from what you do best."

"What's that?"

"Making money, that's what you do best. And I believe that's what makes you happiest."

"I thought you were going to say cooking was what I do best."

"You're good at that too. By the way, did you ever tell the Feds what you're thinking about doing with Constantin?"

"I called the FBI field office downtown on Market Street. I think I was talking to a clerk. I told her about Constantin and what we might do together. She took my contact information and said she'd get back to me. I haven't heard from them. I don't think she believed me."

"That sounds like she dismissed you. I know that hurts your feelings. But please keep in mind, it *is* a rather implausible story. I wouldn't believe it if a stranger told it to me."

Helen's words energized Frank. He arose from his couch and went to his desktop. He turned on two TV monitors, one to Fox Business and the other to CNBC, both at low volume. He began to work on his laptop and his cell phone. He contacted Dmitri Scull, the banker he had foresworn. As he labored, the world news teemed with irony around him. The United States was soliciting oil from pariah states such as Iran and Venezuela; Russia was kidnapping citizens of Ukraine and relocating them to Russia, their grand invasion at a standstill. The former seemed nonsensical for a country with large oil reserves; the latter was an extremely inefficient and dangerous way to reverse population decline, particularly when Russian troops were sustaining such high casualty rates in Ukraine. Frank shook his head in bewilderment and continued his work.

Helen came into his office on the second day of this feverish activity and inquired about it. "What are you working on day and night? I've never seen you this dedicated."

"I'm buying a bank," Frank replied.

"A bank? What do you need with a bank?"

"Think about it, my dear. Vinnie's East Coast colleagues have a bank. Constantin has a bank. We need a bank too. Remember Sutton's Law."

"Sutton's Law? I've never heard of it."

"Willie Sutton was a famous depression-era bank robber. He was arrested and escaped from prison several times. When the press asked him why he was always robbing banks, Sutton said 'because that's where the money is.'"

"Okay, I give up," Helen said. "How does that apply to us?"

"I don't want to be running money through somebody else's bank ... especially with the kind of people we're involved with in this deal. Sutton also said another famous thing. When the press asked him why he always used a machine gun when he robbed a bank, he said 'You can't rob a bank on charm and personality.'"

Helen laughed. "He sounds like the kind of person I would like to have known, but I am still not sure how that applies to us."

"I'll tell you another thing about Willie. When the press asked him if his guns were loaded when he robbed banks, he told them that his guns were never loaded because he was afraid somebody might get hurt."

"This Willie Sutton is clearly a hero of yours, but you still haven't explained why we need a bank."

"We need a bank because all the other players in this deal have a bank. Our bank is in Limassol, Cyprus, with branches in Kazakhstan and Mauritius. We can run money through our bank with very little regulatory supervision. That's what we need if we're going to play the game with Constantin and the East Coast crowd."

"I hope you understand we can't do this with guns. It's stupid to rob banks with guns."

"That is precisely what's changed in the last hundred years. Now you *can* rob banks with charm and personality. All you need is your own international bank and the appearance of wealth. The world is awash in cash right now. It's easier than ever to act like you're rich. And we didn't really buy that bank in Limassol. We're the biggest shareholder and have most of the bank's loans. That's how we control the bank."

Helen shook her head in resignation and decided that she needed to talk to Rachel and Vinnie. Since her pep talk two days ago, Frank had gone from a couch-potato to an international bank robber and money launderer.

Frank was only getting started. "We control the Limassol bank now," he said. "We're putting in new management. We're changing the way the bank operates. We're aiming to be very service oriented. I'm putting Harry Gallanis in as the client service manager. The Russians and the other expats in Limassol are going to love us."

"Harry Gallanis?"

"I've known him since he was a kid. He's the son of a Greek guy who ran a restaurant in St. Louis years ago. Harry's in the banking business. He's lived in Limassol for years. Everybody knows him there. He speaks Russian like a Moscow snowplow driver. And he's got the finesse of an international asset manager. He's perfect for the job."

Chapter 4

Vito and Patsy were reviewing their finances on a weekly video conference in late March. The world of finance was moving so fast that their quarterly meeting no longer sufficed. Their revenue streams were looking good from street operations, various investments, and bank earnings. The only laggard was their waste management acquisition in Chicago. Remote work remained in fashion, and their records showed that waste management income in Chicago had not recovered from the Covid-19 downturn.

"What do you think we should do about Chicago?" Patsy said.

"We're not making progress there, but our waste management operations in New York and south Florida have been hurting too. I think part of it is the transition to remote work. That's really hit our income everywhere with waste management. But there's something else too. I can't put my finger on it, but I think somebody's getting more than his share. I think that somebody is Vinnie Palermo."

"His cut is down to three percent of the take, right?"

"You got it, but he still gets to review and approve expenses and everything else before he gets his cut," Vito said. "If he underreports the overhead, his bottom line is bigger. He gets more juice, and we aren't carefully auditing it. Even though we've got people out there, I still see his hand in our operation. I think we need to send Sammy to Chicago. I want to know what Vinnie's up to out there."

"Sammy knows the Chicago operation, but he's been very helpful in streamlining our bank's operation here and in Nassau. I don't want to lose him. They also know him in Chicago. They may still have a beef with him about what happened to Tony Rags."

"Forget Tony Rags, he's history. Let's send Sammy out there," Vito said. "We can spare him from the bank for a few weeks. I want to find out what Vinnie Palermo is up to. I don't trust him. I've never trusted anybody in the Palermo family."

The Nassau bank, Sunshine Investment Bank, was controlled by the Five Families in New York City and the south Florida faction in Hallandale Beach near Fort Lauderdale. The bank was doing especially well as the pandemic wound down. Deposits from South American drug profits had increased remarkably in the first quarter of 2022. The two mobsters were unsure why, but they thought the death of Tony Ragusa might have helped the bank's credibility. Vito and Patsy had quietly intimated that Ragusa's demise was their doing. That deed had restored confidence in Sunshine's operation with South American drug kingpins, and money had flowed in like a spring tide.

As they concluded the bank review, Patsy said, "By the way, our people at Sunshine say Frank and Vinnie Palermo have taken over Suyu Bank in Cyprus. I think they've thrown in with Val. So much for getting the Palermo family out of our hair."

"Let's hear what Sammy has to say after he's been to Chicago," Vito said. "I'm fed up with them both. If those two are skimming on us, we'll have to make them feel our pain."

Sam Mancuso flew to Chicago with two accountants in tow. They audited the waste management books and talked to the people that Vito and Patsy had installed to run the business. They visited Vinnie Palermo, who had largely decamped the waste management operation to return to his commercial real estate business. They asked to audit Vinnie's books, but he resolutely declined, telling them they were not entitled to that liberty. They inquired about Vinnie's new business direction with warehousing and distribution for remote work. Vinnie was also not forthcoming with any useful information about that venture's profitability. Mancuso returned to south Florida and reported that waste management was still losing money because office buildings in Chicago mostly remained empty. As far as he could tell, Vinnie was not skimming any profits from their Chicago operation, but Patsy and Vito continued to suspect that Vinnie was somehow stealing from them.

❦

The first day of April is known as April Fool's Day throughout the world. It's a tradition that reportedly dates to ancient Rome, but it is so appealing a concept that the world has embraced and sustained it over two millennia. Word jokes, visual pranks and elaborate charades are common, but these deceptions generally aren't practiced by older people. In another painful consequence of aging, elderly people lose their sense of humor. Frank regretted that he had become more serious as he grew older. His days and nights seemed to merge. He slept less and felt less functional during the day. He needed a pill to sleep, a pill to stay awake, and a pill to try to make love to Helen. He also needed a pill for his blood pressure, a pill for his cholesterol, one for his prostate, another for his acid reflux, and two for his arthritis. Frank's daily routine had become a carousel of pills. Simply staying alive was more work than he had ever imagined in his youth.

His increasing wealth further complicated his life. When he lived at Beaumont, he had money, but he didn't think about his money because it didn't seem to matter. His only financial responsibilities as a widower were to help his friend Charlie and keep Beaumont from failing financially. Now he had significantly more money than ever before, and everyone knew about it. People depended on him. Helen needed his protection. Barney was on his payroll. Vinnie and Rachel needed his financial skills and advice. The first of April came and went without Frank giving it a passing thought. World events cried out for concern and satire—inept and corrupt politicians, dangerous tyrants making war and killing in-nocent people, fumbling health authorities posing as experts—all would have begged for ridicule and mirth if they had not made life so dangerous. Frank knew he could not right all these wrongs, but he was determined to try, at least about the war in Ukraine.

Frank summoned his brain-trust to an in-person meeting in early April. Vinnie and Rachel had flown down from Chicago with her dog, Cane, to join Frank, Helen and Barney. A mild day with a hazy sun of early spring warmed them ... not quite shirt-sleeve weather, but tolerable to sit outdoors on the patio of Helen and Frank's house on the bluff above St. Albans. At one p.m., they gathered around antipasto and mineral water. Cane, the Australian Shepherd, took up his sentinel position on the side of the patio.

"Thank you for your help so far with our new bank venture," Frank said. "Let me summarize where we are at this time. We effectively have control of the bank in Limassol, and we've changed the way it operates. The staff is much more customer-oriented now. A friendly bank, can you beat that? The deposits are growing. I am in the process of marinating the money we received from First Baltic in Moldova. We are learning more about Constantin's Moldova bank. Rachel, would you update us on the First Baltic situation, and then I'll talk about the Limassol bank."

Rachel, the reluctant hacker and new bride, spoke tentatively. "We've had difficulty penetrating their files, but as best I can tell, they have very large deposits from a significant number of Russian oligarchs. These deposits are mostly held in Euros, but the bank has been augmenting their depositors' holdings by speculating on big recent swings in the value of the ruble and profiting on the upswing in commodities since the Ukraine war started. The people at First Baltic know what they're doing. I can tell you that."

"Does Putin have money with the Moldova bank?" Barney asked.

"We can't tell yet," Rachel said. "The bank has several numbered accounts that we can't trace to specific individuals. We're working on that. As you know, it's always been difficult to link Putin to any tangible assets. He distances himself from his wealth with layers of LLCs and shell companies. He's very canny about that. He takes care of his ex-wife and his girlfriends. That's pretty easy to trace. He doesn't directly own his yachts or his fancy villa on the Black Sea, but he most likely controls those assets indirectly. The rest of his wealth is a blind alley. However, I believe he can tap the oligarchs' wealth whenever he wants. He's made his three pals from his early political career in St. Petersburg very rich. He keeps them close to him. I'm sure they can provide money to him at any time."

"Do you think First Baltic suspects that someone has penetrated their firewall?" Frank asked.

"I can't tell. We're trying to be circumspect in our searches of their files...make it look like their clients are checking on their accounts. The bank has a very secure electronic system with multiple safeguards and checkpoints. We have to be careful."

"Barney, how are we doing with our security?" Vinnie said. "I'm sure there are any number of people who are interested in what we're trying to do."

Barney smiled. "We are secure as of the present. So far neither your colleagues on the East Coast or Frank's new colleague in Moldova have been probing us. But, Frank, I can tell you that your guy Dmitri Scull is probing us. What do you want to do about him?"

"Leave him alone, but don't give him anything he doesn't already know about us. He's my real-time contact with Constantin. We need him to keep in touch with Constantin on the official level."

"You should be talking to Constantin directly," Helen said.

"I can't do that because Constantin won't deal with me directly. Everything goes through Scull," Frank said. "He keeps himself isolated from almost everybody. Scull is the only one I know who has a pipeline to him."

"And how does he do that?" Helen asked.

"We don't know yet," Rachel said. "Scull has a channel that we can't identify, but they seem to be in fairly constant touch."

"There are still too many loose ends in this deal," Frank said. "In my opinion Scull is a known entity, but Constantin remains a known unknown. We've got to do better at identifying the communication link between those two." Frank took a sip of Pellegrino and ate two arancini balls. "Now let me tell you a little bit about the Limassol bank. We've been washing the money Constantin sent us, and the total amount hasn't deteriorated. In fact, despite its many iterations, it's actually grown a bit. I'm using the south Asian network, and they've been very efficient. I've tried to make the process straight forward and traceable, since it's clean money and mostly ours to start with. We're about ready to return it to Constantin. The Limassol bank has been a good investment."

"How closely does Constantin monitor your activity?" Vinnie asked.

"He's been following the money when it's cash, but he tends to lose it when it goes to crypto because we keep it in small blockchains," Frank said, "then he picks it up again when it converts back to cash. I don't think we've given him anything he doesn't already know. He simply wants someone else to wash the money ... to distract attention from him. He's also trying to learn if we know something about money he doesn't. If we pass this test, he says he'll start sending us his money."

"So ... we're about ready to handle some dirty Russian money. I think we can run it though my business. We'll input it as income from the warehouse leases and output it as losses in the commercial real estate downturn. I think it'll work."

"It'll likely be more money than you could imagine," Frank said. "The oligarchs have sunk tons of money into the London real estate laundromat and into their yachts, art, jewelry and jets, but they've got a lot left over. About a hundred of those thieves control half the wealth in Russia from what I can tell. The war has put their wealth in the spotlight ... and not in a good way. They need new ways to hide their money, and we can help them with that."

"And they are going to be very unhappy when they find out what you intend to do with that money," Barney said.

"We'll worry about that when we start to make it happen. Helen and Moselle have some ideas about how to deflect the oligarchs," Frank said. "Now let's sit back and enjoy the day. Spring is in the air, and things are looking up for all of us. Tonight, we're giving a little party up here to introduce some of our friends around here to the newlyweds."

୧୨

A cold rain began later that afternoon, and the party for Rachael and Vinnie had to be moved indoors. It was a small gathering, featuring Helen, Frank, Moselle, Barney, and a few invited guests from the country club and the Wings Road neighborhood. Frank had laid out plates of antipasto and bottles of Prosecco and a Verdicchio from the Marche region. To please the Francophiles in the group, he put out a bottle of Meursault and a plate of smoked salmon with the accoutrements. Beethoven's Moonlight Sonata played softly on the house sound system. Cane inspected the guests and then retired to the patio to sit beneath the table, sheltered under the umbrella.

The rain seemed to seep into the mood of the guests. Introductions were made, after which the guests clustered around Barney and Moselle, whom they knew. They stared at Rachel and Vinnie but seemed reluctant to initiate social contact. Unmasked, the guests persisted in keeping their social distance from everyone but Moselle and Barney. Helen ushered Rachael and Vinnie around the room, trying to engage the guests in conversation, but to little avail. The party ran out of energy and ended by eight o'clock.

When the guests had departed, Cane indicated that he was ready to come inside. The dog shook off a few raindrops, walked through the great room, and sat by the front door, looking quizzically at Rachel. "Thank you for the party and for introducing us to your friends," Rachael said. "They seem like very nice people."

"Nice is as nice does," Helen said. "We only have a few friends, and I believe after tonight we have even fewer than I had thought. They all acted like they were afraid of us."

Frank turned off Beethoven and put on some vocals by Emilio Pericoli. Helen smiled. "There's your boy singing "Al Di La" again. I think that's your favorite song."

"Not so," Frank replied. "Puccini's 'Un Bel Di Vedremo' is my favorite song, but the opera itself is so ineffably sad. Every time I see it performed, I'm hoping it will turn out differently, but it never does. She always dies at the end. Despite the sad story, 'Un Bel Di' is still one of the most beautiful songs every written. On the other hand, Pericoli always makes me feel young. Our guests tonight made me feel old." He poured himself a glass of Grappa and settled on the sofa with his feet on the coffee table. "One mistake we made was inviting people who live near us," he said. "That drone attack really spooked them."

"Every one of them seemed to come here tonight more out of morbid curiosity than any friendship," Helen said as she looked at Rachael. "I'm sorry for you two that it was such a disappointing evening. We wanted to honor you, and all we did was produce some weird neighbors."

Vinnie joined Frank on the couch with a cold bottle of Peroni in hand. "It wasn't that bad. I met a guy tonight who knows more about warehouse robotics and logistics than anybody we've been working with. I think he can really help us."

"*Très romantique, mon amour.* The honeymoon appears to be over," Rachel said as she helped Helen clear the dishes.

"You'll thank me later, sweetheart, when you see what his ideas can do for our bottom line. I'm going to bring him up to Chicago and have him revamp our distribution and delivery system. And just for the record, in my mind the honeymoon will never be over."

They finished the evening and said their goodnights on the two themes of business success and romantic failures. Rachel and Vinnie would stay over the night before returning to

Chicago. The next morning Frank got a text from Dmitri Scull saying Constantin wanted to have another meeting in New York, again in Central Park. Frank and Vinnie arranged the trip for the next week when Constantin announced he would be in New York. Frank had a foreboding about this meeting and asked Barney to be present discreetly during their time with Constantin in the park. He texted Scull that he and Vinnie would attend the meeting as before. What he did not reveal was that Barney would also be present, posing as a homeless person sleeping on a nearby bench near the meeting.

Chapter 5

The world maintained its weirdness in April. Public health officials and politicians seemed reluctant to admit that Covid-19 was again receding. They advocated a second booster vaccination, and some of them predicted another surge of the virus in the future. They seemed unhappy that other events were pushing the virus to the backburner of public attention. In the United States, inflation, and waves of immigrants on the southern border continued. The senseless war of Russia against Ukraine raged. The Russian military pulled out of their northern offensive against Kyiv, the capital city, and pivoted to the east to try to consolidate their gains in the Donbas region. The Russian withdrawal in the north left a trail of widespread destruction and murdered civilians. The Battle of Kyiv, as it was being called, was hailed as the greatest feat of arms of the still young 21st Century. Western politicians flocked to Kyiv to show their solidarity with the brave Ukrainian people. Photo opportunities with President Zelenskyy of Ukraine were highly desirable, particularly when the background showed the terrible devastation of Kyiv. Amidst this carnage, Val Constantin and his Moldova bank continued to make money.

For their second meeting with Constantin, Vinnie and Frank flew to Westchester County Airport and took a Lyft ride into Manhattan. Barney flew commercial to LaGuardia Airport and took a taxi to 54th Street. He had earlier purchased some clothing from a man about his size at a small homeless encampment at Hampton and Interstate 44 in St. Louis, which he had vacuum-sealed in a plastic bag. He changed clothes in the taxi. The New York cabbie had seen many strange things, but he had never encountered anything like the transformation that occurred with this fare from the airport into Manhattan. When Barney walked into Central Park at 9 a.m., he looked and smelled the part of a street person-- unshaven, dirty, and reeking of urine, sweet wine, cigarettes, and marijuana. He carried a ragged blanket and dragged a tattered roller bag behind him. He lay down on a bench about thirty paces from the presumed meeting place and pulled the blanket over his face. Sleep came easily to Barney. He set his internal clock to awaken at 10 a.m.

Constantin's two men rousted Barney at 9:45 a.m. One pulled the blanket down and said, "Get up, you worthless piece of street shit and move on! We don't want you around here when decent people are meeting."

The full view of Barneys' size made the bodyguards step back. Barney sat up, and they took another step back. He fixed them with his ferocious glare. "Move on yourself, you *mudak*. This is my bench. Can't you see I'm trying to sleep? You want this bench, you're gonna have to pay for it."

Constantin's men moved on, and Barney lay down and again covered himself with the blanket. Constantin arrived and took his seat on the nearby bench ten minutes later. He motioned to his two men. "You need to do something about the derelict over there. Please tell him to leave."

"We tried, sir, but he won't move. He says it's his bench and he's trying to sleep. He looks completely ... how do you say it in English ... wrecked. He's so far gone on drugs and cheap wine, we don't think he'll make a problem for you. We didn't want to have a scene with him."

Constantin shrugged and motioned the two men to search and scan Vinnie and Frank, who were approaching their location. He glanced nervously at the recumbent figure on the nearby bench. "Good morning, gentlemen," he said to Vinnie and Frank. "I'm happy to see you again. Thank you for joining me. Now please let me get to the point. I have reviewed your activities with my first installment, and I think we can work together." Constantin remained seated on the bench with his left hand up to keep Vinnie and Frank at a proper social distance.

"We were washing our own money, and it was clean to start with," Frank said. "That's never hard to do. Let's talk about where we go from here."

"Where we go from here is simple. I send money to you, and you process it. I have learned that you now effectively control the Yusu Bank in Limassol, which I didn't expect. But it is convenient for both of us. You process the money and send it back to me, minus your commission fee."

"Send it to us in small portions," Frank said. "It's easier to handle that way. Large amounts attract undue attention."

"I suggest the first transaction should total twenty-five million Euros. That's the amount we usually process at First Baltic. We'll send it in small transfers. You can process it as you wish. I agree that large blockchains and specie deposits are difficult to conceal."

"Good. We'll wait to hear from you," Vinnie said.

"Will you join me for lunch?" Constantin asked.

"Sorry, not today, but thanks for the invitation," Frank said. "We need to get back home. Vinnie's recently married, and he can't be away for long."

"Yes, I know about that happy event. Please accept my congratulations," Constantin said. "And gentlemen, before we part, let me say one more thing. As you know, this kind of business can sometimes be a risky venture. You should be ready for setbacks and reversals, both financially and to your persons. Now I ask you to allow me a little time to depart, and please don't bother to follow me."

"Wouldn't think of it. Have a good day."

After that vague threat, Constantin stood, gave them a slight bow, and walked toward the park's south entrance on 59th Street. One of his men followed while the other man loitered at the pond's edge some distance away. Vinnie and Frank set out for an east entrance to the park. After a short delay, the remaining bodyguard signaled to two young men, who followed Vinnie and Frank. Barney quietly arose and followed the two followers.

The two young men attacked Vinnie and Frank before they exited the park. They rushed their victims from behind, chopped at their necks and kicked them hard in the but-tocks. It all happened in a few seconds. Vinnie and Frank went down, and the two assailants moved in to apply more kicks. Before that happened, Barney punched them both in the kidneys. The assailants groaned and tried to turn to face the unknown force behind them. Upon turning, Barney threw simultaneous short jabs to their jaws. They went down without another sound. Barney set about relieving them of any weapons and identification.

Frank, sitting up, said, "How did you do that? You were like two people."

"It helps to be ambidextrous. They're lucky there wasn't three of them. I would have had to use my feet too." He came over to help his two friends stand up. "You were right, Frank. You two are running with a fast crowd here."

"What do you make of them?" Vinnie asked as he stood and steadied himself against Barney.

"The two thugs with Constantin looked like Wagner Group operatives who were past their use-by dates. These two brothers on the ground are just local boys trying to make a buck."

"What should we do now, Barney?" Frank asked with a shaky voice. "And thanks for saving our asses."

"I think we need to get moving right now. Constantin's other guy is watching us, and he'll report to his boss. I'm guessing these two locals didn't mean to kill you, but they planned to make you very sore ... maybe break a few bones. For my part, I think I may have busted the smaller one's jaw."

☙❧

Pasquale Salerno and Vito Ragusa had decided to use video conferencing exclusively to review their business operations. It was a new method for them, but their advisors had told them virtual meetings were the present and the future. They both were determined to adopt current technology. Frank's accusations about their misogynistic and backward ways had stung them. They had been inherently cautious throughout their criminal careers, never leaving a definitive trail of their nefarious dealings, which they thought aided their advancement. They often remarked that they had been indicted multiple times, but never convicted. But the world had moved ahead of them. They were determined to show that they could still live and thrive in it. They kept at it although the transition turned out to be a hard slog for them. They were now using modern accounting methods to track their growing assets, but they continued to rely on face-to-face communication to make big decisions. They never used cell phones for business discussions; they didn't issue written orders, and they made only small talk indoors and inside their limousines. The use of a video-conference program for their business raised risks they had always tried to avoid.

They had begun meeting weekly on a secure video link to review the status of Sunshine Investment Bank in West Palm Beach and Nassau, Bahamas. Their bank was bringing in so much illicit South American drug money that they were forced to send more of it to Val Constantin's bank in Moldova for laundering. This development made Frank and Vinnie Palermo's growing association with Constantin's bank important to them. As always, they reviewed the numbers, but they were careful about their language. You never knew when the wrong people might be listening.

"We can't shake off those two," Vito said. "I'll bet old Frank is handling some of our money. Can you beat that?"

"I usually don't care who's handling our money as long as we get it back clean. But I am not working with the Palermo crowd. They've caused us enough trouble already. Now that we're talking about Val, I'm thinking maybe we should deal him out and work with somebody else. Val's cut is getting too high. We're seeing less back from him every time ... says it's all about inflation and increased heat from the EU regulators, but I don't believe him."

"Val's got a big hand in banking and money flow over there," Vito said. "If we find another network, it won't be in Eastern Europe. I think the war over there is attracting too much attention from nosey people. Maybe we should look into Asia ... somewhere down there. I don't know much about that part of the world."

"I'll bet Frank knows about Southeast Asia. His bank's got a branch in Mauritius. That's always been a conduit for money from Asia to Europe. We need to find out more about how he's handling money through that bank. I also want to know more about the woman Vinnie Palermo married. She got into our bank's files before, she might be trying to do it again. We never settled with her. We owe her for what she did."

"You're right about that," Vito said. "We'll definitely have to do something about that. I don't think she's interested in us right now. Our contacts in Belarus think she's trying to hack Val's bank."

"Maybe we could get her to work with us," Patsy said. "Then we could find out what she knows and how she does it."

"Remember this hacker we're talking about is now married to Vinnie Palermo. I don't think she needs money, being married to Vinnie. Anyway, she's too protected by Frank's security."

"Frank's security is down in St. Louis," Patsy said, "Or out in that Podunk place they live now. I can't remember the name of it, saint something or other. We don't know as much about Vinnie's security in Chicago. I think we need to probe him a little ... try to get into his files."

"Old Frank's built a helluva operation. He's got muscle, money, brains, and that crazy gun-toting wife in his group." Vito felt his anger rising and decided to stop the virtual conference before he said something incriminating. "We should continue to talk about this when we get together in person. I don't want to go on about this the way we're doing now. Let's get our friends in Belarus to see what they can do with Vinnie's files. We need to find out if he's skimming on us. I think he could be our doorway into Frank's files."

"It's going to cost us some money," Patsy said. "They're raising their prices ... talking about inflation and all that."

"It's not about money, Patsy. We got plenty of that. It's about information, and that's where we're hurting."

❧

Frank and Vinnie's new money laundering operation began to thrive. Vinnie recorded Constantin's money as income from his warehousing and distribution centers and losses from his commercial real estate operation. Frank laundered the money through his Southeast Asian contacts. They returned the laundered money as cryptocurrency to Val Constantin's Moldova bank via Frank's Limassol bank. Their three percent processing fee was substantial because of the large amounts of the money they handled. When they returned the money to Constantin, they also sent their processing fee directly to the Ukraine government as cryptocurrency. Yet, they considered the arrangement unsatisfactory because of the large amounts of laundered money they returned to Constantin. They needed a more efficient way to relieve the oligarchs of their wealth—a topic that increasingly occupied their attention.

The situation became more complicated on the first of May when two people from the FBI and Treasury Department rang Frank's doorbell in St. Albans. He let them in, checked their credentials and ushered them outside on the terrace. They were Peter Andrews, special agent for the FBI, and Margaret Benson, treasury department senior investigator. Andrews spoke first.

"Mr. Palermo, you are certainly wondering why we're here. A few weeks ago, you notified our field office in St. Louis that you were entering into a business agreement with a banker in Moldova named Val Constantin."

Frank tried to look annoyed. "I definitely contacted your office, and I never heard back. I thought the person I talked to blew me off as a crank or something."

"I apologize for that, Mr. Palermo. Since that time, we have by other means identified considerable transfers of funds between Suyu Bank in Limassol, Cyprus, and Constantin's bank in Moldova."

Margaret Benson jumped in. "Mr. Palermo, we know you are a principal shareholder in Suyu Bank."

"So what?" said Frank. "Limassol is full of Russians. That's why it's called Little Moscow. Many of them bank with Suyu. We try to service all our depositors."

"We don't know all of the particulars yet, Mr. Palermo," said Benson. "Please be aware that we aren't pursuing any action against you at this time. But we do suspect that some of that money belongs to Russian oligarchs. Given the current war in Ukraine, that possibility is a major concern for us."

"What do you want from me? I've tried to cooperate with you from the beginning, and now you show up making veiled threats. I thought you people only dealt with domestic issues.

"Money is plentiful these days, Mr. Palermo," Andrews said. "We try to follow it wherever Americans take it."

"I thought you people had enough to do monitoring terrorist parents at school board meetings."

Helen, who had been recording this conversation from the safe room in the subbasement, jumped up and moved fast. She removed her Sig-Sauer micro-compact from her bra holster, left it on the chair, and raced up to the kitchen. She brought a chilled bottle of Sanpellegrino Limonata on a tray with four glasses out to the terrace.

"I just returned from the club, darling," she said. "It's a warm day and I thought you and your guests might enjoy a little refreshment. May I offer you some sparkling water?"

Andrews and Benson rose. Introductions were made. They each accepted a glass and sat down. Helen noticed that Andrews was studying her carefully … probably trying to see where she carried her gun. Benson seemed oblivious to everything around her except the views of the distant valley and river.

After a few sips and more small talk, Andrews stood and said, "Thank you for the hospitality, Mrs. Palermo. We must be going. Mrs. Palermo, it was a pleasure to meet you. We'll be in touch about your activities with the Limassol bank." He and Benson walked rapidly through the great room toward the front door.

After Helen had seen them out, she returned to Frank, who had not moved from the terrace. "Really, darling," she said, "That was uncalled for. You don't need to make them angry before we know what they want. We're got enough enemies right now without them jumping into the mix."

"I know ... you're right as usual. But those two pissed me off. Turning up here and talking to me that way. I don't think they really know what we're doing, but I'm not taking any chances. We need to armor up and lawyer up. This money thing is getting serious. If the Feds are sniffing around, probably every criminal outfit in Eastern Europe knows about us too."

Chapter 6

A few days later Barney drove a black Lincoln Navigator up Helen and Frank's driveway. The couple, forewarned about the new vehicle, walked out to meet him. "Here's the first one, the other one will arrive tomorrow," Barney said as he handed Helen the key-fob.

"What is it? It looks like a beast," Helen said.

"It's a fully armored SUV—steel plate all around, over and under it. It's got bullet-resistant glass and run-flat tires. It will stop M4 or AK47 rounds. Handgun rounds will bounce off it. Roadside bombs won't faze it. You can be in a major shootout and drive home in one piece."

"Where did you get it?" Frank marveled.

"Vinnie got both vehicles for us. They came from Tony's stable. The Chicago outfit doesn't need them anymore. They're all either dead or in jail. We got a sweet deal on these bad boys. This Navigator can be Helen's vehicle. Frank, you're going to love your Navigator. Your vehicle's got some special features that will let you communicate privately with your financial people. Vinny picked up a third one for Rachel. It's really going to come in handy in downtown Chicago. These vehicles also have some features put in particularly for the Chicago outfit. They're not just defensive. They can fight back too."

"I shudder to think about how much gas these things will drink."

"That's a downside, but you said you wanted to armor up. These behemoths will do that for you. Now we'll need to put some firepower inside them. I can handle that end. How are you doing with the lawyers?"

"I found a good international finance lawyer in Chicago through Vinnie. She's flexible enough to work with us on what we're doing. We've actually lined up several good criminal defense lawyers here in town. St. Louis has a reputation for criminal defense lawyers. I think we're set in that department."

After three days of practice, Helen felt she could handle the Navigator. She drove it to her weekly volunteer stint at Beaumont with Barney riding shotgun for the first time. He had previously followed her in another vehicle and waited for her in Beaumont's parking lot. When they entered the building, the residents greeted Barney with the delight of finding a long-lost friend. They crowded around him and told him everything that had happened since he resigned his position at Beaumont. His reception in the dementia unit was equally enthusiastic. Barney could get more out of the residents with a smile than any of the staff could obtain by any means. When they finished the shift, Helen said, "The manager should pay you to show up. Your do more for the mood of the place than any pill they could push."

"Half of them in the locked unit won't remember I was here by tomorrow. I want to sit in the backseat on the way home. I have a feeling that something's about to happen."

"What do you mean? What's going on?"

"Nothing specific. It's just that too many cars passed us on the way here. There's a lonely stretch on the road before you get to the interstate. Some people might be preparing a little surprise on the way back."

The lonely stretch was about a mile of winding road through a hilly section that had not yet been developed.

As soon as they entered it, they saw a car ahead parked on the roadside with its hood up and a person leaning over the engine. "Speed up," Barney said. "Don't slow down for anything. This looks like a bushwhack."

He scrambled over the backseat, grabbed his rifle, and raised the back window. Another sedan was closing on them from behind. Helen jammed the accelerator. The pursuing sedan came faster; two men leaned out of the rear windows with what looked like automatic rifles. Barney rested his rifle on the back door frame and fired a sustained burst into the grill of the pursuing sedan. He put down the rifle and picked up a smaller weapon. Two men with handguns stood behind the parked car and fired several rounds at the Navigator before diving into a ditch for cover. As they sped by the parked car, Barney held his weapon steady and fired a short burst into the driver-side at tire level. As the Navigator entered a curve, they could see the pursuing sedan immobile in the middle of the road, its three occupants trying to flog the smoking engine with their body armor. The parked car was riddled in a low horizontal line and had two flat tires. Its occupants had emerged from the ditch and were gazing at the speeding Navigator.

Helen slowed down and Barney said, "Keep going as fast as you can. I don't think they'll come after us when we get to the interstate. They still may have some drones over us while we're on this road."

"Who *were* they?"

"Hard to tell, it all happened so fast. The assault rifles looked like AK-47s. That would possibly make them Wagner group operatives. But you never know these days with everybody armed to the teeth."

"How did you know this was going to happen? I didn't see it coming at all."

"Just a hunch. There were too many cars on the road when we came out to Beaumont and way too many people standing around in the parking lot when we left. Three people in that parking lot is a crowd. It didn't look right to me. I'm glad we didn't have to shoot it out in the parking lot. Beaumont would never have signed up another resident after a second gunfight in their parking lot."

"Where did you get your arsenal? I've never seen anything like the guns you were shooting at them."

The Sig-Sauer XM5 is the new squad rifle for the U.S. Army and Marine Corps. It replaces the M4. The Rattler is the new personal defense weapon for special ops personnel. I put these weapons in all three vehicles we bought from the Chicago outfit. Vinnie's security people are familiar with them. I saw to that."

"Okay ... I'm not making myself clear. What I'm trying to say is *how* did you get those guns?"

"I helped develop and evaluate them. It was a little side gig I had with the Pentagon when I was working at Beaumont. I happened to acquire a few during that process. These two weapons have just been selected by our military after rigorous testing against other candidate weapons. They haven't been widely distributed to military personnel yet."

"I think I need to learn how to handle those weapons."

"What about Frank? Shouldn't he get involved with this?"

"Frank hates guns. Let him do what he does best. Please teach me how to handle these weapons. Our situation is clearly becoming more dangerous for all of us. I can be useful the next time this happens, and I'm sure it will. Frank can't do this sort of thing."

ℝ

The next day Frank convened a meeting of the little band of conspirators. Frank, Helen, Barney, and Moselle in St. Albans were joined by Vinnie and Rachel in Chicago on a secure video link.

"Thanks to everyone for being available on short notice," Frank said. "I think you all know about our visit from the Feds and the shootout near Beaumont. That's yesterday's news. I'll get back to what I think it means. First, I'd like Rachel to bring us up to date on what's happening with the Moldova bank."

The video screen shifted to Rachel. "We also received a visit from the FBI and Treasury here in Chicago. We're not sure how much they know. But they seem to be sniffing around Suyu Bank in Limassol. As for First Baltic, our progress has been slow. Their electronic firewall repairs itself every time we penetrate it. One thing I can tell you is their deposits are growing daily. I also think they're making a fortune hedging on the volatility of the ruble."

The screen shifted back to Frank. "Constantin never seems to lose money, no matter what he does. The ruble is becoming more valuable. I'm sure he anticipated that. What worries me is our involvement with crypto. We've had great success using it to hide money, but the whole idea of stable digital money seems to be collapsing. Every time we buy crypto, it's lost value when we try to convert back to cash. The crypto market is going nowhere but down right now."

"Will it come back? What do you think?" Vinnie asked.

"I don't know," Frank said. "The death of crypto has been predicted before. It's an attractive concept, but nobody has been able to make it work. The problem for us now is we can't use it for our purposes. I think Constantin is in the same bind...but that leads to a bigger problem for us."

Nobody spoke because they knew where Frank was going. "The small fee we get for washing money for Constantin is just that...it's too small. We need a big score. We need a way to take big money from the oligarchs in a much bigger way and quickly."

"We know their assets are trapped in Russia, right?" Barney said. "They're all tied up in commodities like oil and gas."

"They seem to be selling their oil to India and China," Helen said. "And they're transferring it at sea to cover their tracks. The sanctions don't seem to be tying them down much, and Europe is still dependent on their natural gas despite all the brave talk."

"I'm thinking we should work on a plan with rare earth metals," Frank said. "Give it some thought...something with manganese, lithium, cadmium...maybe even nickel. I think we need to get the oligarchs to put their money into a plan to export the metals to countries that can make the batteries. Russia doesn't have the know-how to do that, but they have the raw materials."

"So, the oligarchs get even more money," Moselle said. "How does that help them if they can't put it somewhere?"

"But they can put it somewhere," Frank said. "They can put it in Suyu Bank."

"I'm beginning to see the framework of where you're going with this," Helen said. "We'll not only have every criminal element on three continents and the Feds after us, we'll also have Putin and his private army against us. What could possibly go wrong?"

"That's the point," Frank said. "If it works, it has to happen quickly ... very quickly. The money goes to Suyu and then to Ukraine before anybody can stop it."

Rachel who had been quiet throughout the video conference joined in. "Frank, uh...I know you're Uncle Frank now, but I still think of you as Frank if that's okay. I respectfully think we're in a little over our heads here. We're trying to hatch a scheme to take in multiple oligarchs at once. These guys are very sophisticated. Governments have been trying to get their money right and left. Everybody else is after it too. They can spot a money grab or a scam a mile away."

"What do you suggest then, Rachel?"

"I think we should concentrate on the Constantin connection. This is preliminary information, but we are beginning to think the Moldova bank is Putin's main conduit to the West. And we're also pretty sure that there are two

Constantin brothers--Valentin in New York and Vladimir in Moldova. We've been dealing with Valentin in New York."

"So, there *are* two of them," Helen said. "That explains how they can operate so well on two continents. If we're really getting into this thing, we need to go after those two. The oligarchs are dying like flies, and it's not all suicide. If those two are running Putin's money, forget the oligarchs. Putin will kill every mother's son of them if they don't cooperate. We need to go directly to the source ... bend Val and Vlad. Or even better bend one and work him against the other one."

"You never cease to amaze me," Frank said. "And how do you think we could bend one of them?"

"Money ... it's always about the money. You run your rare metal scam on Val. He'll suck Vlad in, and then we give them both a haircut ... and maybe the other Vlad in the process."

"That might actually work, Rachel said. "They're both struggling with the collapse of the crypto market. Washing money is getting more difficult for all of us. If we gave them a new angle to make money, they might actually bite."

"I think we need to talk to Vinnie's friends in New York and South Florida first," Frank said. "Those boys have been washing money through that Moldova bank for years. We need to get them on board, or they'll tip the Moldova people about what we're doing."

"Actually, Patsy Salerno is saying they want to talk to us," Vinnie said. "And they'll come to us. We can set up a meeting in St. Louis if that's okay with you, Frank, or we can do it remotely. I think they're getting interested in our commercial real estate operation. And just for the record, they're not my friends."

"We should do it here. I want to see them in the flesh when they start lying. They can choose as many as they want to watch on a remote link, but I want them here in person."

ço

The meeting occurred one warm June afternoon on Helen and Frank's terrace before the oppressive summer heat arrived. Patsy arrived with a newcomer, a man he introduced as Pauli Leone, a representative from the New York families. Barney's security people had thoroughly searched and scanned the two before showing them to the terrace, where the two St. Louis couples were already seated. They were joined by Vinnie and Rachel, who had flown down from Chicago. Introductions were made, and they all found seats under a large sunshade. A mild breeze from the northwest improved the ambience.

"Where's Vito," Rachel asked innocently.

"He went to college," Patsy said.

"Oh, that's nice. What's he studying?" Rachel's question ended with a soft gasp. Vinnie, seated beside her on a loveseat, had jabbed her ribs with his elbow.

"Tax law," Patsy said, glaring at Rachel.

"He means that Vito has taken a little vacation on Uncle Sam's dime," Vinnie said. "I didn't know about it, Patsy. Can you tell us what happened?"

"The new federal prosecutor in Chicago said we had a problem with unreported income from our waste management operation up there. Vito copped to a few months and a large fine to keep it all quiet. Otherwise, the Feds would have been deep into our books. We didn't want that. Waste management is complicated."

Frank changed the subject. "Vinnie says you're interested in commercial real estate in Chicago. Can we talk about that?"

"What we're interested in is what you and Vinnie are doing. Commercial real estate is in the tank. Nobody wants to go to work. They all want to stay home and work off the internet. We have to hand it to you, you saw this happening before a lot of us did. We want to assume a position in your warehousing and fulfillment operation."

"How much do you want?" Vinnie said.

"We'd have to see your books, of course, but we're thinking about a quarter stake. We'd like to study your operation from the inside. We're not trying to take over, you understand. We just want to learn what you're doing and take it back to the East Coast. We're particularly interested in your distribution and delivery software."

Barney, who had been silent up to that point, jumped in. "Mr. Salerno, please hear me on this. Mrs. Palermo and I were attacked on a road in south county about two weeks ago. It was a professional ambush. Do you know anything about that?"

Patsy looked surprised. "I don't know nothing about any ambush. Was anybody hurt?"

"No bodily harm," Helen said. "But Mr. Browning here fully depreciated at least one of their vehicles."

"Well, I'm glad nobody was hurt. I don't know nothing about this attack you're talking about, but I know it didn't come from us. I swear that is the truth."

Everyone except Pauli had been intently studying Patsy's reaction to Barney's question. Pauli seemed fascinated with the towboats and barges on the distant river. Patsy's calm demeanor and measured speech betrayed no advance knowledge of the attack. He seemed genuinely surprised.

Frank nodded to Vinnie, who said, "We're glad to hear it, Patsy. We need to work together. We'll sell you a piece of our operation, but we need something from you."

"What's that?"

"We need you to stop doing business with the Moldova bank," Frank said. "We can show you other ways to move your money around. The Moldova bank's gotten very risky because of the war in Ukraine."

"You seem to know a lot about us, Frank. We've worked with that bank for years. They run a real good cleaning service."

"Not anymore," Vinnie said. "They've been doing it with cryptocurrency. You can't depend on crypto anymore. You're losing real money every time you buy crypto now. We'll show you how to clean your money using small African and Asian banks. You get to keep your money and maybe even make some more at the same time."

"So, what's the deal?" Patsy said.

"The deal is simple," Vinnie said. "We sell you a piece of our business, including a license for our warehousing and distribution software, which is proprietary. You'll make a ton of money duplicating our operation on the East Coast. We'll also show you how to clean your South American assets. Your part is to stop doing business with First Baltic. What's not to like about that deal?"

"I'll have to think about it." I'll have our technical people talk to your people."

"It's not a standing offer. We'll need an answer in five business days. The world situation is changing rapidly."

"What does that mean?"

"It means you're losing money while you're thinking about it."

Chapter 7

The war in Ukraine upstaged the Covid-19 pandemic in June, but the virus persisted. New subvariants of Omicron emerged that were highly infectious and largely evaded vaccine protection. They were not especially virulent except in the very elderly or immunosuppressed. Government officials continued to urge vaccination, and drug companies worked to update vaccines. None of the experts seemed to want to acknowledge that the vaccines did not protect against infection with the new variants. What physicians called Long Covid was another phenomenon, characterized by persistent shortness of breath, dry cough, malaise, fatigue, joint pains, and other complaints. What recovering patients called "brain fog" seemed to involve mild confusion and problems with short-term memory. Exhaustive testing usually revealed no abnormality, and no treatment proved effective for Long Covid other than time.

In Ukraine, the warfront became static in the east, settling into an artillery and missile duel. Russian forces launched rockets at cities, inflicting widespread destruction and horrific civilian casualties. It was a particular Russian way of war perfected over centuries by Tsars, Stalin and now Mr. Putin. Grain remained siloed in Ukraine with the Russian Black Sea blockade. A global food shortage loomed. Russia cut off natural gas supplies to countries it deemed unfriendly and reduced supplies to other European countries, citing maintenance problems with the Nord Stream pipeline. July 21 loomed as the pivotal date when Russia said it would resume full gas flow in pipeline. Most people believed the Russians would stall on their gas delivery contracts and use energy as a weapon. When July 21 arrived, Russian President Putin announced that gas would flow but at a reduced rate. He blamed the problem on Canada's failure to repair turbines used on the pipeline, a claim that was widely disputed. All of Western Europe feared a total Russian gas cutoff in the coming winter. No expert dared predict how the Covid-19 virus would behave in the colder months.

In the Midwest, government officials continued to track the financial manipulations of the Palermo family. Peter Andrews of the FBI and Margaret Benson of the U.S. Treasury Department met weekly about what they called the Palermo Case. Peter had grown up in the Midwest and had worked in the St. Louis office for years. Margaret Benson had recently been transferred from Treasury's D.C. headquarters, expressly to investigate money laundering operations out of Chicago and St. Louis.

"It looks to me," Peter said, "like they're stealing from the oligarchs and giving it to Ukraine."

"They're breaking the law," Margaret said. "Our investigation supports that conclusion. We've got to report it."

"I know." Peter said. "But I think we should cut them a little slack ... see where they're going."

"We can't do that. Where they're going should be straight to jail." Margaret's pedigree was New England wealth, prep school, Ivy League, Yale Law. She had chosen government service and she meant to be successful. She knew that bringing down a money laundering operation of this magnitude would establish her as a force at Treasury.

"We can watch them for a little while. Think about it. If they're stealing from the oligarchs and giving it to Ukraine, isn't that what we want?" Peter was a Midwestern farm boy, who had worked his way through a state college and law school. He knew he had advanced as far as he ever would with the Bureau.

Young Margaret was only beginning to climb the career ladder. "If we go down for this, it's on you. I hope you know what you're doing."

"Let's just give it a little more time," Peter said. "This thing will break very soon. It won't be pretty, and it won't be on us. We're watching seals swimming with sharks. I'm telling you it won't end well for the Palermo clan."

∾

Patsy Salerno and Pauli Leone also studied the finances of the Palermo family. Vinnie and Frank weren't made men. Vinnie was on the fringe of the organization; Frank was on the outside and liked it there. Patsy and Pauli both considered Frank to be a nonentity. Vinnie was the operative force in their minds, but the uncle and nephew were bringing in prodigious amounts of money. This fact alone made Frank interesting.

"I'm telling you I don't trust that crew in Chicago," Patsy said. "You know what I mean?"

"Looks like they've lawyered up pretty good. I think we should hit them both," said Pauli, whose MBA from Fordham had not restrained his temper or reformed his judgment.

"They always seem to know what we're doing. I can't figure it out unless they've hacked us again."

Frank's an amateur ... and he's old—totally over the hill. But he's got a smart-ass wife. What's her name?"

"Helen Palermo," Patsy said. "Tony Rags used to call her Annie Oakley ... said she was a crack shot. It's Vinnie I'm worried about. He's sneaky smart, and he's put together a good crew."

"Who do you think went after the woman and her bodyguard two weeks ago?" Pauli said.

"I don't know. I don't even know if they're leveling with us. I just know it wasn't us."

"Then who was it?" Pauli was persistent.

"Could've been Val or one of his crew. He's in tight with Wagner. Vinnie says there are two of them ... brothers. One's back in Moldova. Maybe it was somebody we don't know about." Patsy was counting the days until Vito got out of prison. Pauli irritated him.

"I know you think I'm just a kid, but I think Vinnie's right this time. We stop using Val. We move our bank over to Road Town. The British Virgin banking people are more friendly to us. But we still got to clean the money somehow."

"Frank can help us with that," Patsy said.

"You trust that old man?"

"I don't trust nobody, but I can feel the heat in Nassau. I agree ... we got to move the bank. And you need to lay off Frank. He's taught me a thing or two."

"See, I can come up with a good idea," Pauli said. "I was right about the bank. You got to listen to me more. I've been to college."

"Wrong college. They didn't even teach you what to do with money. Now listen to me on this. I want you to keep a close eye on the Palermo crowd. I think this thing's going to pop ... and very soon."

∾

Frank began to talk about his plans with rare earth metals and batteries. He first outlined the scheme to his little band of co-conspirators ... giving them few specifics, only generalities about moving the metals from Russia through Kazakhstan and then to India where batteries would be made with new technology. He mentioned it casually at the country club and on the golf course. He talked about it with his local bankers and his bankers in Limassol, Cyprus. He and Helen set up a website called battery storage technology, B ST.com, touting the development and commercialization of the breakthrough developments with Lithium-Iron-phosphate battery technology. He created an LLC with the same name. His bank in Limassol with its branch in Kazakhstan would facilitate the finances, and he would be the lead investor in the new venture.

Helen knew even less about batteries than Frank, but she scripted his conversation and the new website. Helen was a wordsmith with a sales scheme. Jamie Madden, the grifter and forger of renown, also lent his skills to their endeavor.

The sore need for new battery storage technology attracted a groundswell of interest. Frank deflected most of the inquiries, but when Dmitry Skull from Frank's local bank left a message, he returned the call the following day.

"Mr. Palermo," Skull said, "thanks for returning my call. Val Constantin is very interested in your battery plans. He would like to talk to you about this."

"Good to hear from you, Dmitry. Have him contact me directly. We're very busy here."

"He would like to meet with you at the usual place in New York City."

"That's not possible right now, Dmitry, but he can come to us. I know he likes fresh air. We can meet at a state park just down the road from our place. Have him call me."

"I'll ask. You know he likes to do things on his terms."

"I know, but times have changed. You can tell him we don't consider Central Park to be safe anymore."

Two days later, Vinnie, Frank and Barney met Valentin Constantin, Dmitry Skull, and a tattooed stranger in the picnic area of Babler State Park in St. Louis County. The six of them sat down under a shelter at 9 a.m., an early hour to minimize the stifling heat and humidity of a St. Louis July day.

After preliminary greetings, Frank began. "Thank you for coming. I apologize for the heat, but I hear it's hot everywhere. I assume you'd like to talk about investment opportunities."

"First, I'd like to thank you for your help with the small African and Asian banks," Constantin said. "The cleaning process is slower than our previous method and there's some leakage. However, it's working for us and we're grateful for your help. With that word of thanks, we'd like to learn more about your progress with batteries."

"You've seen the website," Vinnie said. "I assume you've also checked the links we sent you. The new battery technology is proprietary, but our colleagues in India have made remarkable progress with Lithium-Iron-phosphate storage. These new units hold a much denser charge without overheating. Our operation is vertical from the metal mining to the finished product. It's also scalable—from vehicle batter-ies to commercial power storage. It's the future right in front of us."

"We're interested and would like to get involved," Skull said, "but we're concerned that there is very little informa-tion out there about what you're doing."

Frank smiled. "Check with Davi Nara in Bangalore. He's heading up our research and development end. I'll give you his contact information. We're inviting a small group of fa-vored investors in the initial stage. We'll eventually enlarge the investment pool ... maybe eventually take the venture public."

"How much do you want from us?" Constantin said.

"Let's start with a hundred million," Vinnie said. "We can go from there."

"We control considerably more resources than that."

"We know you do. Let's call it the first installment. That amount should prime the pump for you and establish good faith between us. You should see an immediate return on investment. The conventional battery production is up and running in Bangalore as we speak. The new technology is in the beta test phase now."

"How will the exchange of assets work?" Constantin asked.

"Your installment should be deposited in our bank in Limassol or Kazakhstan," Frank said. "Your return will go to your bank in Transnistria. I assume that works better for you than your bank in Chisinau. You can receive it in U.S. dollars, Euros, rubles or store it as one of our new nonfungible tokens. The NFT is redeemable in any specie in either Limassol or Kazakhstan."

"You seem to have thought of everything," Constantin said. "I'm surprised you know about our bank in Transnistria."

Frank smiled and did not comment. After an exchange of contact and banking information, they all stood and bowed as the meeting ended. Constantin, Skull, and the silent stranger took their limousine back to town. The meeting had lasted thirty minutes.

On their ride back to St. Albans, Vinnie said, "Do you think they bought it?"

"What's not to buy? The more conventional Lithium-ion battery operation is up and running in Bangalore. Our new Lithium-Iron-phosphate breakthrough is mostly theory at this point. They can't prove it wrong because they'd be trying to prove a negative. Anyway, they've got a big problem and they know it. Their old money washing operation is down the tubes. They're desperate, and they need new places to put their ill-gotten wealth."

"You'll have to give them some money back to make this thing work."

"I've got enough of that, and I can't take it with me. My energy investments have soared in value. I've already set enough aside to take care of Helen. We humans are herd animals, and we like to graze on greenbacks. Constantin is no different from the rest of us in that respect. I'm giving him a big field of green to nibble on."

"You didn't bring up the attack on Helen and Barney," Vinnie said. "You didn't ask Constantin about his brother."

"It had to be them, and the brother, if he exists, is irrelevant at this point."

"And who the devil is this Da Nara in Bangalore?"

"Davish Naratha is our man in Bangalore. He runs our money dispersal operation to small Indian banks for us. He recently bought a small battery factory over there with my help. He's the perfect shill for what we're doing with the battery scheme. He's smart and he's the king of patter."

"You trust him?"

"He'll work with us as long as he's making money."

"Frank, you're dealing with a bunch of dodgy people all over the planet," Barney said. "I'm worried they can't be trusted."

"To run this scheme, we need a large network. We've got to take a few risks in this deal. First, we get a big chunk of the oligarchs' money. Then we worry about what comes next."

"I'm pretty sure the third guy today was one of the goons that assaulted you two in New York. I think he recognized me. We've got to be careful with these people."

"And I don't know anything about your network," Vinnie said. "What do I do if something happens to you?"

"It's all in the cloud, Vinnie. If I don't check in with the cloud program every second day, all the encrypted information is downloaded to you. That way you're protected until you need to take over."

Vinnie shook his head in resignation. "You know Rachel's pregnant?"

Frank was nonplussed. "No, I didn't know that. Congratulations."

"We can't put her out front on this. If this scam blows up, every crook in God's creation will come after us big time. Putin's private army routinely kills women and children. Hell, the standing Russian army seems to be doing the same thing."

"Does Helen know?"

"I don't think so. You're the first person I've told."

"Let me talk to Helen about this. This complicates things. You're going to need extra security. Hell, we're all going to need more security."

When the three men returned to the bluff-top house in St. Albans, they found Helen, Rachel and Moselle sitting in the great room in animated conversation. Helen was drinking a Prosecco; Rachel and Moselle were drinking orange juice. Frank noticed that everyone was smiling.

"Okay, what's up?" he said. "I just learned that Rachel is expecting, but something else is going on. You three girls look like the cat that swallowed the canary. And congratulations to you, Rachel."

"These two beautiful women are going to be mothers," Helen said. "Isn't that wonderful? And you and I are going to be godparents twice over."

The two expectant mothers radiated enthusiasm and joy. Helen was clearly happy with this new adventure although she had never born children. The two fathers-to-be smiled sheepishly and kissed their wives. Frank was the only somber person in the room. He felt new burdens pressing down on him at a time when he already sensed he was overcommitted.

Chapter 8

August brought new developments with Covid-19 and Mr. Putin's war in Ukraine. Severe infections with the new viral subvariants continued to decline. In response to this development and to the upcoming school year, authorities relaxed recommendations about masking, quarantines, social distancing, and the need for vaccinations. The experts finally seemed to be recognizing the benefits of natural immunity from previous infection. What the colder months would bring continued to be a puzzle. The public in general had already decided to ignore the virus and try to return to some semblance of a pre-pandemic life.

The war in Ukraine shifted from the east to the south of the country. Sabotage of Russian military and energy installations in Belarus and Crimea testified to the long reach of the Ukraine military. Negotiations to release grain shipments from Ukraine ports across the Black Sea allowed a trickle of grain to reach Turkey by ship. The Ukraine military, newly armed with precision Western artillery and rockets, began to inflict heavy damage on Russian ammo depots and command structures. A counteroffensive by Ukraine's military to liberate the southern port city of Kherson seemed eminent. The world watched and concluded that invading Ukraine was a bad idea. The Germans had learned this hard lesson eighty years earlier, and now the Russians were learning it too.

Mr. Putin's disastrous war against Ukraine and oppressive Western sanctions caused wealthy Russians to seek other outlets for their money. They recognized that Frank and Vinnie's new battery venture presented a lucrative opportunity for them to profit secretly. Frank primed this pump with his own money, sending it to the bank in Transnistria disguised as profits from the battery scheme. Such a rapid return on investment attracted an ever-increasing amount of Russian money.

When Frank and Vinnie checked the weekly income from the battery operation, Vinnie said, "I don't believe this, Frank. You're running a pyramid scheme where you take their money and donate it to a good cause, and you turn around and give them your money. I've never heard of anything like that. I think it's unprecedented."

"Helen gets the credit. She scripted the website and our sales pitch. She's a genius with something like this."

"What I'm saying is your money won't last forever. Then what're you gonna do? You can set it up like a classic Ponzi deal and give the oligarchs some of their money back. That could stretch this thing out."

"No way. The oligarchs' money goes to Ukraine and nowhere else. We've got to close this thing out in the next month. The oligarchs are slow ... and they're desperate, but they'll figure out what we're doing in a few weeks. We've got to get their money *molto veloce*. That means less than one month in this case."

"That's all the more reason to set it up like a traditional Ponzi scheme. You can easily return a little of their money if this thing is going to close down in a month."

"I'll only do that if I run out of my money. Right now, I want to send all the income from the battery project straight to Ukraine."

❦

Unbeknownst to Patsy, Pauli continued to use the bank in Moldova to launder South American drug money that came through their bank in the British Virgin Islands. They both were close enough to Val Constantin to know that a prodigious amount of the Russian oligarchs' money was flowing from the bank in Moldova to Frank's bank in Limassol, Cyprus.

"What the hell you think is going on with Frank's bank?" Patsy asked Pauli.

"I think he's running a scam. He's got a battery scheme going on ... says he's got the inside scoop on some new battery technology. He's running it out of India. He's got a website with links to all kind of scientific stuff. It all looks bogus to me."

"These Russians are smart ... and they're rich. You think they'd fall for a scam like that?"

"All true, but they're in a bind," Pauli said. "Their assets outside Russia are tied up with sanctions and seizures. Their cash in Russia can't go anywhere. They need to make money somehow, and it looks like old Frank is giving them exactly the 'somehow' they're looking for."

"Old Frank running a con on a bunch of Russian billionaires ... imagine that." Patsy had a low opinion of Frank, but he distrusted Helen and feared Vinnie. "Find out if this is really going on and if Constantin is putting any of our money in this thing," Patsy said. "If they're skimming our money, we're gonna have to talk to Frankie boy."

"How do I do that?"

"How do I know? You're supposed to be the smart guy. That's what you're always telling me. Find out where the money goes once it gets to Frank's bank."

"We're pretty sure we already know where it goes, Patsy. It goes to an outfit he set up called the Ukraine Reconstruction Fund." Pauli had his own hackers in Belarus, and they had stumbled on Frank's scam by following the circuitous flow of Russian money out of Suyu bank.

"To Ukraine? He's stealing from the oligarchs and giving it to Ukraine? You've got to be kidding me."

"As best we can tell, that's what he's doing. He's also giving some of his own money back to the oligarchs."

"You telling me he's running a Ponzi scheme with his own money? That's the craziest thing I've ever heard. You don't do that. You run a Ponzi scheme with your mark's money."

"Well, Patsy. That's what it looks like he's doing. I'm not kidding you."

"I'm impressed, Pauli. You're finally helping us here. This may be our ticket to shut Frank and Vinnie down. They've been a step ahead to us since before Tony Rags passed away."

"It also looks like they laundered some of the Russian money through Vinnie's real estate operation in Chicago. They stopped that a few weeks ago."

"Do the Feds know about this crazy con?"

"I don't think so. At least I don't think they know about the battery scam. They've got taps and probes all over the place, but I don't think they've been able to find out everything about what old Frank's doing."

Patsy smiled because he saw a weakness he could exploit. "Then tip them ... and tip Constantin too. Make sure they don't know it's us. It's time to put some heat on Frankie boy and his whacko operation. The Feds can do our work for us ... shut him down. And if they don't do it, Valentin and his Wagner boys will do it. I'm sure Frank and Vinnie are stealing money from us. I just can't figure out how they're doing it. Maybe along the way we can boost some of that Russian money too."

∞

The Constantin brothers were difficult to track because they communicated by satellite phones on an encrypted hookup.

Valentin in New York talked daily to Vladimir in Chisinau, Moldova. Billions of Russian rubles were flowing through their bank in Chisinau to Frank's Bank in Limassol, ostensibly to finance new battery technology in Bangalore, India. The brothers were getting money back through their branch bank in Transnistria ... money they thought was a return on investment from the battery operation. They had no idea what Frank and Vinnie were really doing until Pauli Leone's people tipped Valentin. At first Valentin didn't believe the tip because it sounded so preposterous—that Frank would send Russian money to Ukraine and give them his own money. But as Valentin's security people carefully traced the flow of money through Suyu bank in Limassol, it became apparent that the tip was true; Frank and Vinnie were stealing money from Russian oligarchs and giving it to Ukraine.

Valentin was forthright when he talked to Vladimir in late August. "They're stealing our money and giving it Ukraine, Vlad. I'm pretty sure of it."

"I checked the links you sent me," Vladimir said. "That's what it looks like. I still don't believe it. Why would he do that? If it's a Ponzi scheme, all he has to do is return a little of our own money to keep it going."

"It's the closest thing to an altruistic scam I've ever heard of ... if there is such a thing. What do you think we should do?"

"You'll be the one in extremis if this thing blows up, Vlad. Tell me what you think we should do. We've dug a deep hole for ourselves."

"We obviously have to shut them down, but when we do that, we'll be in trouble with our investors. Putin's friends and enemies keep dying. I'm having trouble telling who's who around our fearsome leader these days. The one thing I'm sure about is somebody's killing them, but I have no idea who it is. I simply don't want us to be on that list. I think I need to come to America and talk to these Palermo people."

Valentin was certain that his brother wanted to get out of Moldova. "Certainly, come on," he said. "We'll set up a meeting with them right away. They're working mostly out of St. Louis these days, and we'll have to go there."

"I thought they were running things out of Chicago."

"It's changed. I'll fill you in after you get here. Everyone over here seems to be working from home. I think old Frank's home is easy to defend. It's up on a hill. He's got really good security, and I hear his wife likes to shoot people."

"I've heard about her. I'm on my way."

"And Vlad, bring some portable wealth when you come. We may need to put some pressure on the Palermo crowd, and it's going to cost us."

∽

Frank assembled their brain trust at his St. Albans home in early September. They had stopped using video conferences because Rachel feared they were too easy to hack. They met under a shaded conference table on the patio early on a Monday morning. Vinnie and Rachel had flown down from Chicago, and Moselle was free to attend because the country club was closed on Monday.

Frank thanked them for coming and began with a summary of the battery operation he was running out of Bangalore, India. "It's really going better than I expected," he said. "Money is pouring into Suyu Bank from the oligarchs, and it's all going straight to Ukraine. Harry Gallanis is doing a great job over there."

"And you're giving them your money to juice this weird operation," Vinnie said. "Maybe you could explain it to all of us. That's the part I don't understand."

"It's a no-brainer, dear nephew. If we run it like a classic Ponzi scheme, they'll figure it out even quicker. This way, I can send my money directly to them from Bangalore, and they'll think the battery operation is legitimate ... at least for a while."

"It'll work as long as your money holds out. Anyway, I'm glad we stopped washing the Russian money through my Chicago business. The Feds were beginning to sniff around with what we're doing."

Frank turned to Rachel, "Can you tell us what our friends in Moldova are doing these days?"

"So far, they don't seem to suspect that we're monitoring the accounts at First Baltic. We've noticed recently that Vladimir Constantin is preparing to fly to New York. That's news because he rarely travels abroad. A short trip to Transnistria is a big deal for him."

"That means he'll want to meet with us. Please let me know when he leaves Chisinau. I'm not going to New York. We can meet here at the house or at the state park if he wants fresh air. I'm betting he won't return home once he gets out of Moldova. What about our friends in New York City and Hallandale Beach?"

"They're busy with their usual nefarious machinations on the local level. On the international scene, they've just about finished moving Sunshine Bank from Nassau to Road Town. The bank being in Road Town seems to be attracting much more interest from South American drug interests.

We think they'll come after your battery money once they're fully set up in Road Town."

"I hope we'll have completed the battery money transfer before they make their move on us. How's the security picture coming along, Barney?"

"We've put in better defenses against drones. The neighbors haven't budged on beefing up security at the subdivision gate. They're saying if we can't live like civilians, we should move out and start a military-style operation somewhere else."

"How's target practice going, Helen?"

Helen glared at Frank. "I've pretty much mastered the XM5 and the Rattler out at our remote firing range. Barney's been very helpful with both weapons. I love that little Rattler. We'll definitely be ready to start robbing banks after you've given away all *your* money."

"My dear, I've put aside enough money for you to live comfortably once this thing breaks open. You have nothing to worry about."

"I get to worry about you, don't I? I'm entitled to that worry! Or maybe that doesn't count. Maybe you're trying to get yourself killed ... all of us killed. And what about Barney and Moselle and new baby Browning? What about them when you go broke?"

Frank knew he had touched a raw nerve and tried to change the subject. Helen would have none of it. "Frank, darling, I think you've lost your way on this. Let governments and big charities rebuild Ukraine. You don't need to be doing this. You're putting all of us in danger that we don't need."

Barney jumped in at that point. "Don't worry about us, Helen. We've got enough money no matter what happens. I think the important thing now is to close down this battery scheme without going to jail or bringing down Putin's private army on us."

The meeting of the brain trust ended on that point—everyone unhappy and fearful for the future. Frank's plans had not changed. He was still determined to drain money from the oligarchs.

❦

Peter Andrews and Margaret Benson held their weekly meeting on their money laundering probe every Wednesday. Midweek worked best for them because Margaret always flew to Washington to report on Monday, and Peter took Fridays off, trying to grow grapes and make wine on some land he bought in Ste. Genevieve County south of St. Louis.

This arrangement meant they only worked on their probe three days a week.

"We know what they've been doing," Margaret said at their meeting in late August. "We know how they've been washing dirty money through the nephew's business in Chicago. We need a full-fledged raid—seize all their papers, phones, laptops and hard drives, the whole nine yards."

"Why don't we make a social call first?"

"What are you talking about?"

"Simple. We make an appointment, and we just drop in, you and me. We tell them what we've got on them. They can't make that evidence go away. Then we tell them we're looking for help to make the case on the mob and the Russians ... tell them we're open to make a deal."

"Why do you want to do that?"

"Simple again. All we have on them now is the dirty foreign money they ran through the nephew's business in Chicago. They did that for about a month. Then they stopped. They evidently figured out we were on to what they were doing. We need their help if we want to nail the Russian gang and the mob in this deal. You need to look at the big picture here."

"Peter, I'd like to bring down the mob and the Russians in this thing as much as anyone, but why do you think the Palermo family would help us?"

"We tell them we'll go easy on the illegal money laundry they've been running if they help us with the mob and the Russian connection."

"You're basically saying we blackmail them."

"Not blackmail, Margaret. We make a deal with them. We use a small fish to catch two big fish. We do that all the time in the Bureau. Think about it. We're sitting on a goldmine of international corruption here."

"I think you're playing me again, Peter. I don't know much about baseball, but I can recognize a curve ball when I see it. If we do what you're talking about, we could end up with nothing."

Chapter 9

September saw Covid-19 recede further from the public mind. Governments and the media continued to stress death rates, need for vaccinations and other aspects of the pandemic. The new bivalent vaccines were designed to protect against the original virus and the recent variants of Omicron. These new vaccines were widely touted, but they were slow to become available. Confusion abounded on the actual efficacy of the vaccines and whether the new vaccines were better than the originals. People had been told earlier that the vaccines would prevent infection. That assertion turned out to be false. Vaccines were emphasized for young children, who rarely had severe infections. Parents worried about the long-term side effects of vaccinating young children. Masks were advocated for children in some schools and not in others. Given the conflicting information and recommendations, the public lost confidence in the pronouncements of experts. One fact seemed to hold up--severe infections and deaths tended to occur in the elderly and immunosuppressed. Younger and healthier people might get infected, but they usually recovered.

Other factors tended to push Covid-19 from public consciousness. Inflation continued to hammer away at wage earners. The southern border remained porous. High government officials sounded clueless or worse. People tried to put the Russian war against Ukraine out of their thoughts, but events intruded. Ukraine military brass had been talking for months about a big southern counteroffensive around Kherson. The Russians took them seriously and moved more troops and materiel south from the Kharkiv region. The Ukraine military then launched a counteroffensive in Kharkiv. Russian forces were routed and quickly beat a disorganized retreat. In a replay of their Kiev retreat, the Russians left a trail of destruction and dead people behind, some their own troops, but also many civilians. Ukraine regained most all of the Kharkiv region and threatened Luhansk. The world cheered Ukraine's military progress and recoiled at Russian atrocities. In response, Russian President Putin called for a mobilization of reserves and new conscripts. Tens of thousands of Russians fled the country to avoid conscription.

Helen and Frank watched television footage of mass graves outside the newly liberated city of Izyum. "Here we go again," he said. "This is just like what happened at Buchan. They destroyed the town, shot up the locals and stole everything in sight."

"It's ugly, darling. I can't imagine what they're thinking. Do they really believe they're killing Nazis?"

"I'm not sure any of them are even bothering to think. They're poorly led and equipped ... free to rape, kill and steal at will. Reports say the entire Russian army in Ukraine is drunk. If I were younger, I'd go over there and volunteer to fight for Ukraine. I hear thousands of people have already done that. I've asked Rachel to double down on probing First Baltic Bank and the Constantin brothers. In the meantime, the least we can do is take money from the oligarchs and send it to Ukraine. This battery storage scheme is doing a pretty good job of that."

"You'd better close the battery deal down fast, darling, before the sky falls on us. I sense that circumstances are closing in as we speak."

"We're just about there, my dear. I'm meeting with the two Constantin brothers soon. I think they're coming around to our way of thinking."

"And what does that mean?"

"It means they're going to cooperate with us … help us loot the oligarchs as much as possible, and then live quietly in a very remote place."

"Why would they do that?"

"They'll take a substantial cut of the battery investment money before it comes to us. As you keep saying, it's always about the money."

☙

Vladimir Kostokovich Constantin definitely wanted out of Moldova. He had seen too much, primarily in the Russian-controlled neighboring region of Transnistria, and he had heard a great deal more. His beloved Russia had deteriorated into a criminal dictatorship that had looted the entire country, even the military. Vladimir had a numbered account at Sunshine Bank in Road Town, BWI, courtesy of his business associates in New York City and south Florida. He also possessed several passports. All he needed was a quiet exit from Chisinau, and his brother, Valentin, had arranged that.

Val met him when he arrived at JFK Airport from Frankfurt. They embraced and kissed, brothers who had not seen each other since before the pandemic. "You had a good trip, I presume," he said when they were settled in Val's limo.

"It was a little hectic in Frankfurt. I haven't traveled in a long time. I'd almost forgotten how to do it."

"Anyway, you're here. You brought some portable wealth?"

"Yes, hard carbon sewn into my suit coat."

"Good, my Wagner colleagues like hard carbon. It's nearly as good as gold and much easier to transport. The three I've hired are a despicable, unreliable lot, but good help is hard to come by these days."

"If Prigozhin kicked those three out, I'm appalled to think you hired them."

"As I said, good help is hard to find. No one wants to work on any terms."

"When do we meet with the Palermo people?"

"I've arranged a plane to take us to St. Louis as soon as you're rested."

"Why don't they come to us. I don't want to go out there like a supplicant. That's not a good way to start."

"They won't come to New York. They say the city is too dangerous."

"Then let's do it tomorrow if they'll see us on short notice. I have no time to rest at this point. Events are racing along in my part of the world."

"I'll set it up as quickly as possible. Our Wagner associates might not be available tomorrow. They like to freelance."

"They're your associates, not mine."

☙

Vitorriano Santorelli Ragusa was released from an upstate New York prison on September 23 after a three-month confinement. It wasn't much of a prison—more like a rundown Holiday Inn surrounded by razor wire. The prison was designed for nonviolent offenders and featured two cafeterias, an exercise room, lounge, movie theater, and ample outdoor space for walking and relaxing. The only thing the establishment lacked was wine and Grappa. Vito soon remedied that deficiency with help from a cooperative but expensive corrections officer. Vito passed his three months in relative comfort. He slept well and kept track of family business with weekly visits from his consigliere and accountants.

Vito had copped a plea for tax evasion for unreported income from his newly acquired waste management outfit in Chicago. The plea deal, accompanied by a large fine, enabled him to serve three months and return to his operation in

Queens, New York City. Sicilians, like many other people, objected to paying taxes. Sicily had been overrun by invaders since time immemorial. They had been ruled by distant overlords who wanted their bounty and gave little in return. Politicians and bureaucrats in Rome currently ruled them, which explained why many of them had come to America. Their new country offered more wealth, but they still objected to paying taxes. Vito was certainly of that opinion.

On his first day back in the office, Vito examined the books with his consigliere and two accountants. Vito shook his head. "This is crazy. Pauli Leone dealing with First Baltic behind our backs. On top of that, he has been siphoning off money from this battery investment scheme the Palermo clan is running. Can somebody explain this to me? Can somebody explain what is wrong with Pauli Leone? That boy is supposed to be smart. We wasted our money sending him to college."

His two accountants sat attentive and silent. They knew Vito was processing information at this point by asking rhetorical questions. They would be ready when Vito wanted to discuss the specifics of money. His consigliere helped Vito use his tablet computer.

"It looks here like Vinnie and Frank Palermo have sent over a billion dollars to this Ukraine Reconstruction Fund. Is that fund legit?"

"We have every indication that it is, sir. The money goes straight to the government in Ukraine."

"And we sit by while Pauli runs his little side gig on the Palermo money. That wasn't our agreement. What the hell am I missing here?"

"Sir, we kept our part of the bargain. Vinnie Palermo has licensed his warehousing and delivery software to us. That's greatly increased our profits in our commercial real estate effort here on the East Coast. In return they asked us to stop doing business with First Baltic Bank. They also helped us find new ways to process money that didn't involve First Baltic."

"And you complied with their request to stop working with First Baltic?"

"Yes sir, we did. The entire agreement has greatly worked in our favor. However, we think Pauli has continued to work with First Baltic without our knowledge."

"So, you're telling me that Pauli has been taking some of that money when First Baltic sends it to the Limassol bank. How has he been doing that? And while you're thinking of that answer, tell me how Pauli continued to work with First

Baltic behind our backs. That's another question you're going to have trouble answering. Get Pauli in here!"

Pauli sauntered in with his hands in his pockets, an insolent grin on his face. "Welcome back, Mr. Ragusa. We've missed you."

"Well, I haven't missed you, Pauli. As of right now I'm sending you back to the street. You're a capo again, and that's all you'll ever be. You blew your golden chance to be a team player while I was away. You can pick up your old crew and do some real street work. That's about the limit of your leadership talent."

"What just a minute, Mr. Ragusa. I've done well while you were away. Both the waste management and commercial real estate operations are making money. I don't understand why you're doing this."

"First of all, I'm doing it because I can. I don't owe you any big explanation, but I'll give you a hint. You broke our agreement with Vinnie and Frank Palermo when you continued to work with First Baltic. In addition to that, you've been taking some of the money that First Baltic's been sending to the Limassol bank. How did you do that?"

"I don't know what you're talking about, Mr. Ragusa."

"Don't play me for a fool, Pauli. Tell me how you siphoned off that money."

"Pauli was unsure whether the acting boss was bluffing or knew what he had done. He decided to tell the truth, an unusual strategy for him. "I'm sorry, Mr. Ragusa. Our hackers in Belarus found the money trail from First Baltic to Limassol and then to Ukraine. It was convoluted but we finally figured it out. I talked to Val Constantin and told him we were on to what he was doing. I told him we would keep quiet if he sent a cut to us."

"Us? Who is us?"

"Our organization. Our bank in Nassau."

Your memory is bad, Pauli. The bank is now in Road Town, British Virgin Islands. You were the one recommended we move it. You've set up a secret account for your stolen money, and you can't even remember where the bank is. You had no plan to share the money with our organization. Now get out of here or you'll be a soldier, not a capo."

Pauli Leone slinked out. The location of their bank was a serious memory lapse. He was furious to be embarrassed by an old man in front of smart accountants and clever lawyers. Vito Ragusa had crossed the line. Pauli planned revenge of some sort. He decided to attack the Palermo family. They were the cause of his troubles with the organization.

"Now get me a video conference with Patsy Salerno," Vito said. "I can't believe he was part of Pauli's little shit show."

❧

Russian military setbacks in Ukraine accelerated the flow of money from the oligarchs into Frank's battery investment scheme. The rapid progress of the counteroffensive by Ukraine in the Kharkiv region and the looming liberation of Kherson in the south caused Russian President Putin to call up reserves. This resulted in a mass exodus of draft-eligible Russians in every imaginable direction—to Mongolia, Kazakhstan, Georgia, Belarus, Finland, Norway, and Poland. Two men even fled to a remote Alaskan island by boat. The exodus not only involved people but also Russian money, a considerable amount of which went into the battery investment scheme. This development caused Frank to summon his brain trust.

"Thank you all for coming here on short notice," Frank said to his group. "I was afraid to do this by video conferencing. There are too many unwanted eyes and ears joining in. I have distributed a summary sheet to each of you. We'll burn the sheets immediately after the meeting. Please do not photograph them with your phones."

"Take a few deep breaths and try to relax, darling," Helen said. "We're on your side in this thing."

The others laughed. Frank knew he was being overly cautious. "I'm sorry," he said. "I know I've been stressed with this thing ... we all have. The amount of money we raised was unexpected. We've sent almost two billion dollars to Ukraine. You can see it on the summary sheet. I've sent over a hundred million back to our Russian investors. Of that amount I don't know how much the Constantin brothers kept."

"Make that a hundred million of your own money," Vinnie said. "I'll bet the Constantin brothers have most of it."

Rachel spoke up. "First Baltic Bank has seen a great deal of Russian money go from them to the Limassol bank and to other offshore destinations. We can't tell the total amount because they're handling so much right now. The outflow changes by the hour. The bank is also holding about seventy-five million in new accounts. We think that's your money, Uncle Frank. We think they're dribbling the other twenty-five million of your money out to the oligarchs. Their little branch bank in Transnistria has been quite busy."

Barney gave a soft whistle. "Looks like the Constantin brothers are taking a large service fee. You got any money left, Frank?"

"Not much, Barney. Helen has her trust fund."

Helen and Moselle shook their heads and stared at Frank as they would a deranged man. Frank knew he could not defend himself with any of the three women around the table, especially Helen. He too had been shocked by the amount of Russian money that had flooded his Limassol bank. "I know what I've done seems strange to you, but I felt I had to do something to help Ukraine. I'm too old to go over there and fight. I had no idea how much this thing would grow when we started it."

"Ukraine is a distant place we've never visited with names we can't pronounce. It does seem strange, darling. I think I need to start monitoring your medications. Maybe you should get some psychotherapy."

"Very funny, Helen. We're going to shut this thing down. I'm meeting with the Constantin brothers in a few days. We'll settle up with them. We'll also have to share a little of the battery money with Vinnie's friends in New York and south Florida. We know Pauli has already been getting a piece of the action. I think we've got enough information to embarrass the two Feds who keep sniffing around. We'll use their own faltering to fend them off. It'll all be over soon."

"Frank, I admire your confidence," Vinnie said, "but we've got the Wagner Group, the American mob, and the federal government all after us. I'll have our lawyers talk to the Feds about our tainted money problem in Chicago when the time is right. We can threaten to litigate that and then probably settle for a big fine. The Wagner Group and the mob won't be so easy. They both think we've wronged them. Even worse, we've shamed them in public They'll want money and a pound of flesh."

Frank turned to Barney. "How are our defenses? Can you give us a quick summary?"

"We've got better drone defenses—electronic jamming and laser pulses. You know how our neighbors frowned on us when we used guns to shoot them down...never mind the laws against doing that. We still have a security problem at the front gate. We've tried to beef it up, but the neighborhood association says we can live here like civilians or move elsewhere and set up a military style operation."

Chapter 10

October brought more widespread availability of the new bivalent vaccines against the Covid-19 virus. The new vaccines combined RNA to make the spike protein from the original virus and from the Omicron variant. Early studies had shown little difference between the new vaccine and the original. Both were effective in reducing severe disease and hospitalization, but not infection. The American FDA also approved the new vaccine for young children. The public seemed unimpressed. Few people took the booster vaccine and even fewer gave it to their young children.

Inflation continued to ravage paychecks. Criminals seemed to act with impunity while law enforcement stood by. The southern border remained porous. Debate about abortion reached new political heights. President Biden promised to make legalization of abortion his first priority if his party retained control of Congress after the midterm elections. Beneath this overt turmoil, people grew even more anxious about the prospect of nuclear war. As Russian political fortunes declined in Ukraine, President Putin intimated even more strongly that he would use any weapon at his disposal in his special military operation. Explosions heavily damaged the Russian bridge connecting continental Russia to Crimea across the Kerch Strait. The culprits were unidentified, but Russian pundits named Ukraine. The Kremlin responded with heavy bombardment of civilian targets in Ukraine by cruise missiles and drones.

The Constantin brothers found that physical proximity worsened their political differences. Valentin in New York City fully supported the Russian invasion of Ukraine. Vladimir in Chisinau had come to oppose it. "We need to get out of the banking business in Moldova," Vladimir said. "We're caught between Russia and the West. Money is flowing mostly in one direction, and that's to the West. We're going to be in big trouble with the Kremlin and our rich clients when this all comes to light."

"We've done very well as the intermediary," Valentin said. We're making money on all the transactions. We've made incredible profits on the rise of the ruble. I don't understand your reluctance to continue."

"Don't you see, Val? What we're doing is wrong. What the Kremlin is doing is wrong. They invaded a sovereign country and have behaved brutally when they were not welcomed with open arms."

"Ukraine is not a sovereign country! It's been a part of Russia for a thousand years. What happened in Moscow thirty years ago was a historical aberration. Ukraine has no more right to exist separately from Russia than Texas has a right to exist separately from the United States."

"I find it ironic that you would lecture me on the history of a country that you obviously detest. The United States has enriched you, Val. You live a luxurious life in New York. You have a luxury apartment in the Turtle Bay neighborhood that puts you close to those corrupt politicians at the U.N. They need your services to launder their ill-gotten riches. You eat in fine restaurants ... have a chauffeur and a private jet. You live in a cocoon of wealth and leisure."

"You've lost your way, my brother. You've been isolated in Chisinau too long. You're out of touch with the ways of the world."

"I'm close enough to the world to see how the Russian military operates. They control Transnistria. They assassinate people publicly. Families disappear. Everyone lives in fear. What they're doing in Ukraine is even worse."

"Vlad, war stories out of Ukraine are what Americans call fake news. Ukraine has totally controlled what people in the West hear about our special military operation. We are welcome in the four provinces we annexed in the east. The people there are happy to be Russian again."

"You haven't seen what I've seen, Val, and I've heard about even worse things. Oh, and just for the record, the Russian military has already been kicked out of two of those oblasts. I want out!"

"If that's what you want, it can be arranged. After all, you've become redundant. I can be you with minimal effort."

"You can never be me."

"Well, you'll never know, my dear brother. But let us not argue about my lifestyle. You're out of Moldova and free to pursue a new life. Let us celebrate. May I follow you down to my wine cellar? I have a special bottle of Chateau Angelus I'd like you to taste. It's the last of my 2005s. I think it is near its peak."

Vladimir Kostokovich Constantin never tasted the fine wine his brother offered. Valentin executed him from behind with a single shot to the base of his skull on the last cellar step. The weapon of choice was an 1895 Nagant revolver, the very model of gun Yakov Makhailovich Yurovsky had used a century earlier to execute Tsar Nicholas II and his family. Valentin's tastes ran to expensive antiques, and his pistol certainly fit that bill. He kept the beloved gun holstered beneath his right shoulder during the day. At night he kept it on his bedside table. Following the single shot, Vladimir's lifeless body pitched down the last step to the floor of the cellar.

Little blood was shed. Two of Val's Wagner retainers stepped forward from a side room and wrapped the body in opaque plastic.

"That was a great shame," said Valentin Kostokovich Constantin, "but the time had come. My beloved younger brother has served Russia well. Unfortunately, his enthusiasm had begun to wane." He motioned to the two men, "You know what to do with his remains. But first remove the diamonds from the lining of his coat and put them in the wall safe. You can take your usual ten percent. All the stones will be yours after you have done one more task for me."

The two Wagner rejects started at Val and his brother's body in silent wonder. Conversation was not their strong suit. They waited for Val's instructions before disposing of the body.

"It's the fiery furnace for my late brother. I want to avenge myself on the Palermo clan for what they've done to me and my country. Pauli Leone and his imbecilic associates won't do anything about the Palermo people. We are going to kill their women. Perhaps then they will know who I am and respect me."

❧

Peter Andrews of the FBI and Margret Benson of the Treasury Department finally seemed near an agreement about how to proceed in the Palermo money laundering investigation. Margaret wanted a simultaneous raid on Vinnie's business in Chicago and Helen and Frank's bluff-top abode at St. Albans, preferably done at dusk for the enhanced visuals. Margaret could already see herself as she faced the television cameras and described her takedown of a major money laundering operation.

Peter was more subtle. He argued for an informal conversation with Frank and Vinnie about their misdeeds followed by an attempt to recruit them to snare a mobster or two and nearby elements of the Wagner group. There had been much back and forth between the two federal agents, most it on encrypted federal devices but enough of it exchanged on unsecured personal devices to make their disagreement evident to whoever could eavesdrop on them. Among those listening in were Rachel's team of hackers.

Peter and Margaret met at the Federal Courthouse in downtown St. Louis in late September. After another long session, an apparent agreement emerged. Peter tried to summarize. "Then I think we are agreed," he said. "We'll get a warrant and then pay Frank a visit. If we don't get his cooperation, we'll arrest him on the spot. I know a federal judge in Illinois who will help us. Do you have a weapon, Margaret?"

"I keep a small handgun in my shoulder bag."

"Do you know how to use it? You take it to the range?"

"I fired it a few times when I requisitioned it. That wasn't too long ago."

"Have you ever shot anyone?"

"No ... have you?"

"I think the answer to both questions is no. You should take your weapon to the range and become more comfortable with it. A sidearm is no good if you don't know how to use it. I'll get the warrant. You set up the meeting with Frank. It will be easier for us if Vinnie is there with him when we meet."

Peter arranged for an arrest warrant charging Vinnie and Frank with wire fraud and laundering foreign money through Vinnie's commercial real estate business in Chicago. The evidence was persuasive from bank records and surveillance intercepts that showed the movement of the tainted money through Vinnie's business over about a month. The federal judge in Illinois was helpful as predicted.

Armed with this warrant, Margaret called Frank and requested a visit in St. Albans at a time when Vinnie was in town. She told him they had some new information on banking irregularities in Chisinau. They would either obtain cooperation from the Palermo clan to ensnare the mob and the bankers in Chisinau or they would arrest both Vinnie and Frank on the day of the visit. The plan was a compromise that failed to completely satisfy either of the federal operatives, but it was the only plan they could agree on.

❧

Pauli Leone had two anger levels. The first arose from his poverty-stricken childhood and his dependence on the organized criminals who had taken him in and financed his education. That anger was low-level and constant. He found it useful to motivate his daily work. The second and higher level was intermittent and driven by adverse events. His humiliation by Vito Ragusa triggered this level. Pauli Leon was furious and plotted violence. He knew Tony Ragusa had attempted to attack the Palermo compound in St. Albans with armed drones. He would succeed where Tony Ragusa had failed. He recruited two followers on the periphery of his organization and a drone expert who had a cache of explosives from South American drug sources. They planned to fly a stealth drone armed with enough explosives to level the house above St. Albans. The drone operator assured Pauli that the explosion could be made to resemble an explosion from a natural gas leak.

Pauli's men assembled on the floodplain of the Missouri River at midnight in late October. They tested the drone at low level. All systems seemed to be working. The drone would fly the package of C4 explosives directly into the target house on the bluff across the river. It would also feature a direct video feed to the operators and to Pauli as he sat in his car five miles away in the commuter parking area at Interstate 64 and highway 94. The anxious chatter between the operators and Pauli increased as the moment for launch neared.

Across the river Barney Browning monitored their activities from his house. His stealth sensors in the trees surrounding the floodplain had detected the intruders as they tested the drone, sending alarms to Barney's control center. He also could listen to their chatter from directional microphones he had placed in the trees. Barney had awakened Frank, who joined him in the control center.

"It looks like they're testing a drone," Barney said. "I can't make out the faces but they're three of them. Only one of them seems to know what he's doing. I'll bet Pauli is behind this. He thinks he can do it better than Tony. He always acts like he has something to prove."

"You think they're about ready to launch?" Frank said.

"Looks like it. We'll try to jam it once it's airborne. If that doesn't work, we'll go with the lasers. That's plan B."

When the drone had risen about forty feet above the operators, Barney jammed it with two radio beam guns he had concealed in the nearby trees. The guns utilized radar-aiming and accurately homed on the large drone. The disabled drone briefly hovered and then crashed directly onto the operators. Luckily, the explosives did not detonate, but the shrieks and cries of the threesome directly below the drone indicated their fear of imminent obliteration. The operator and his two assistants raced to their vehicle and fled, leaving the smoking drone on the bank of the floodplain. Five miles away, Pauli immediately knew what had happened when his television feed went black.

"Bingo," said Barney. "That's a drone defense that actually worked. We should drive over there and retrieve what's left of their drone. I think we can learn something about what they're up to. At least we can retrieve the explosive package before somebody finds it and an accident happens."

After the debacle down by the river, Pauli devised another plan. His hackers had told him that Andrews and Benson were planning to meet with the Palermo family. He also knew that Val Constantin was planning to assassinate the Palermo clan. He saw a way to get into the house on the bluff. "Here's what we do," he told his two associates. "We follow the Val's people up the hill to the house. We muscle our way in, disarm them, and pop everybody. I'm ready to hit all the Palermo clan in this deal. They've ruined my life. I'm going to ruin theirs. And I don't care who gets in the way."

"Let's say we get in and do what you say, Pauli. How do we get out? They have a lot of security up there."

"I have a plan for that. I'm going to set it up so we just walk right in like we were invited."

"And how are you going to do that?"

"I know Val is planning to hit the Palermo family. He's going to lure their security away from the house. We follow his shooters to the gate and tell the guard we're invited up there for a meeting. I've been up there. That old man at the gate doesn't know his ass from a hole in the ground."

"So, let's say you get in. How do you figure we get out?"

"We just drive out after we've done the job. It's no problem getting out. I've been up there. The problem is getting in."

❧

Valentin Constantin knew he had to get the Palermo security team away from the compound for his revenge to succeed. He called Frank and said, "Mr. Palermo, I want to meet with you and your nephew at that state park where we met before. You remember it? I want to discuss further cooperation with you regarding our banking practices and our personal security. You might want to bring your security team."

"Yes, I do," said Frank. "Why my security team? I assume this is a friendly meeting."

"Perfectly friendly, but these are very insecure times. Strange things happen when they are least expected. I'm beginning to feel like a Kremlin target. You know I have a brother."

"Yes, I do," said Frank. "Is he coming to the meeting? I'd like to meet him."

"I'll try to have him come. He's even more reclusive than I am. The important thing is that we meet. I have a proposition to put to you. We want to get out from under the thumb of the Kremlin. It will require the cooperation of your security people. Their chief is Mr. Barney Browning. Am I correct?"

"Yes, again. Can you tell me more about what you have in mind?"

"Only at the pavilion in the park can I tell you. This matter should be discussed outside in the open air. Thank you for taking my call."

Frank put down his cell phone. "I smell a rat. We'll leave half our security here and take the other half to Babler. I don't trust Constantin."

Two days later, on approaching a covered picnic pavilion at Babler State Park, Frank and Vinnie saw immediately that the meeting had gone wrong. Val Constantin was alone, sitting at the picnic table studying his cell phone. "Where's your brother?" Frank asked as he and Vinnie stopped about twenty feet from Val.

"He was unavoidably detained. A slight headache ... he suffers from migraine you know."

Frank raised both hands above his head, the prearranged signal to Barney that the meeting was flawed. Barney and two of his men scurried back to their Navigator to return to

St. Albans. One man stayed with Frank and Vinnie, but at a distance beside a leafless sycamore tree.

Frank and Vinnie began to back away from Constantin. "You've crossed me for the last time, Val," Frank said. "If you put my family and friends in danger, you'll be very sorry."

"You've given our resources to those rebels in Ukraine, you stupid old man. You and your foolish nephew have cheated me and my clients. I should kill both of you right now."

"You could kill us, Val," Vinnie said, "but direct your attention to our man over there with the XM5 rifle. He'll shoot you and he's good at it. He won't kill you, but he'll wound you in a way you'll wish you were dead."

Val Constantine stood stock-still under the picnic pavilion as Frank and Vinnie walked backwards to their Navigator. When they were shielded behind the two front doors of the vehicle, their bodyguard walked slowly to join them, still with his rifle trained on Val. Once inside the Navigator, they raced back to St. Albans.

Chapter 11

On a cool morning in late October, Peter Andrews and Margaret Benson stopped their gray Ford sedan at the security booth below the gated community atop St. Albans. They told the attendant, a retired deputy sheriff from St. Louis City, that they were expected at the Palermo house. Helen had already notified the attendant, and they were admitted.

Pauli had expected to follow the Wagner operatives up the bluff. Waiting in the parking area of the little village, he saw a better opportunity. The occupants of the gray sedan might be the two federal agents. They offered an easier chance for entrée. Pauli and his two henchmen followed the gray sedan up to the gate.

"We're with the car that just came in," Pauli said. The gate attendant looked at the three men in a black Chrysler 300 and was mildly confused, but he admitted them.

Following them at another discreet distance, came the three Wagner retirees in a green Jeep Cherokee. They wore green slacks and turtlenecks. "We are security for the meeting," said one of them in stilted English that almost sounded American.

By this time the gate attendant was mildly alarmed, but he admitted them also. He made a mental note to call the Palermo residence for confirmation, but several other residents of the subdivision arrived in quick succession. His friendly banter with people he knew caused him to forget the call.

In this way, the three vehicles snaked up the bluff toward the Palermo-Browning compound, the occupants of each largely unaware of the intent of the others.

Peter rang the doorbell. Helen was alone but she expected them. They had texted her they wanted to visit with news of their investigation. She figured they were lying as usual, but she knew she could handle the two of them. Frank and half of their security team were all off to Babler State Park to meet with Val Constantin and his elusive brother, Vladimir. Helen had sent their three remaining security personnel down to the inn in the village to guard Moselle and Rachel.

She admitted the two federal agents and directed them to the great room. Before she could close the front door, Pauli Leone and two men in black, ill-fitted suits barged into the house. The newcomers each carried a Benelli M2 short-barreled shotgun. Helen had no choice but to direct them to the great room and introduce Andrews and Benson.

Pauli feigned mild surprise by the presence of the federal agents. Helen insisted that he and his friends stay. When she returned to close and bolt the front door, three tall, gaunt men with multiple neck tattoos stood in the vestibule holding PP-19 Bizon automatic weapons. Since they didn't shoot her immediately, Helen invited them into the great room. This motley collection of eight hostile people found seats and glared at each other.

Helen kept the XM5 and the Rattler in the hall closet to deal with outside hostiles. How she regretted not being able to access her weapons at a time like this.

Helen had acted in regional theater in Omaha for many years before she married Frank. Early in her career she fancied herself a classical actor and had pursued Shakespearean roles. She hadn't been very proficient at Shakespeare, and producers and directors had agreed with her. When classical roles grew sparse, she had gravitated to more contemporary roles, but she still aspired to do Shakespeare. She had never forgotten the lines from many of his plays. Lady Macbeth struck her as vicious and ultimately weak, Desdemona as only weak and compliant from the start. Juliet was a naïve child. On this singular morning, Helen knew that she had to conjure up strength and wile to survive the situation in her great room. Shakespeare had some strong women in his plays; Beatrice and Portia came to mind. Helen narrowed her azure blue eyes until they appeared pale blue. She put on her wire-rimmed glasses and inserted her earpiece, connecting her to Barney and his team outside.

"I see everyone's here," she said, standing in the middle of the great room. "Let me begin with you three men in green, since you're the latest arrivals and the most heavily armed."

The three Wagner Group rejects sat impassively, their automatic weapons across their laps.

"I'm sure you came here to kill Frank and me and are surprised by the number of people waiting in line. You three are recently of the Wagner Group. We know your names and we know your history. We have documentation of what you did in Buchan and in Africa. You're no longer in the Wagner Group because of that. Now you're freelancing for a very dodgy bank. Before you think you have nothing to lose, remember your presence here is recorded and already in the cloud. Also, please be aware that we have attached your bank accounts in South America. You can walk out of here alive and get your treasure back or we can splatter our insides all over this elegant room. Think about it."

The three ex-Wagner operatives shifted uneasily, still with their fingers on the triggers of their weapons.

Helen smiled at Pauli. "I hope you don't mind me calling you Pauli. I'm wondering if Patsy knows you and your associates are here. I've watched you and Patsy muddle along since Vito went off to prison. The only smart thing I've seen you do is move your shady bank to the British Virgin Islands. You're losing money every day dealing with the Moldova bank, and you think you're smart with your fancy college education and all that. Whose side are you on, Pauli? Tell me that. It's time to make up your mind!"

The three mafioso sat sullenly, their shotguns across their laps. Everyone ready to shoot, but no one daring to go first.

She turned to Andrews and Bennett. "And what are you two here for? Did you come to arrest Frank? You may have a warrant, but what you've done is bring a piece of paper to a gunfight. You didn't bring enough firepower. We've got your e-mails and texts. We can show the world how you've argued and vacillated. It won't look good for your career, Margaret, when this comes out."

After a short silence, Margaret Benson said, "You think you can intimidate us, Ms. Palermo, but you're wrong. You and your accomplices have laundered stolen money through a reportedly legitimate U.S. business. You've taken it from sanctioned foreign sources and sent it to other sources abroad in abrogation of U.S. laws."

"Pretty words, Margaret, and I admire your chutzpah. Please remember you've come to a gunfight with a warrant, a mere piece of paper. If you and Peter here, who seems to be much brighter than you, come out of this alive, we'll welcome the opportunity to litigate your allegations. But until that time, let us return to the more immediate matter of your survival."

Helen raised her arms and twirled in a pirouette. Her slow rotation was sufficient for everyone to see she had no weapons. She picked up the remote and turned on the big screen television. A click on the outside security cameras revealed Barney Browning and five other figures surrounding the house, kneeling in firing position with weapons pointed at windows and doors. "You can see Mr. Browning outside with his men. They have guns too, and their guns are much better than what you brought to this party. You can put down your weapons and walk out of here with no prejudice from us, or you can experience the immediate consequences of a very bad decision. You six with the big guns, put them down and walk out now!"

After a silence, Pauli was the first to put his shotgun on the floor. His two associates followed. The three Wagner retirees then put down their weapons. The six would-be shooters rose and moved toward the front door.

"They're coming out, Barney. Let them go. I promised them safe passage." Helen glared at Andrews and Benson. "You two may also leave now, but remember I just saved you from certain death ... and not a pretty one at that. Now put your weapons on the floor. You can always come back another day to retrieve them when we don't have so many guests in the house. Until then, we'll keep your guns here. You'll simply have to report that you've misplaced them and are looking for them."

Andrews removed his standard issue Glock from his shoulder holster and placed it on the floor. Benson hesitated for a moment and then removed a little Sig-Sauer nine-millimeter handgun from her shoulder bag. They walked slowly toward the door.

Helen spoke as Andrews opened the front door for Benson. "We'll show you where to find the three Wagner operatives. You can detain them if you're interested. Of course, that depends if you have time to spare from trying to arrest us and pursuing all your other important domestic investigations. I know you've been awfully busy with the parents at the school board meetings."

Margaret Benson paused at the door. She turned and opened her mouth to speak, but Helen interrupted her. "We'll also show you how to find the Constantin brothers. But if you come after Vinnie Palermo, Margaret, remember what will happen to your career aspirations."

After the eight visitors had found their cars and departed, Frank rushed into the house and embraced Helen. "We didn't want to shoot first," he whispered. "It was too risky with the number of people around you. I heard what you said to them. You avoided a massacre. Are you okay?"

Helen's body was shaking, and her voice cracked. "It may have been my finest hour on stage. I tried to channel the Bard's most heroic women. I was so scared I almost wet my pants. Don't ever leave me alone like that again. I had the XM5 and the Rattler in the hall closet, but I had no way to get to them. They took me by surprise. They all seemed to barge in at the same time."

"I'm so sorry, my dear. They misled us and we fell for it. We thought we had a chance for a deal with the Constantin brothers ... turns out only one of them showed up and he wasn't interested. Barney figured it out quickly, and we came back as fast as we could. Please forgive me."

After Helen had stopped hyperventilating and collected herself, Frank said, "Your monologue was brilliant, my dear, but I'm not sure everything you said to them was accurate."

"I was making some of it up. It just had to sound convincing. I figured those Wagner thugs had their money stashed in several places. It turned out I was right about South America. They had no way to check their bank accounts in real time. If they had reached for their phones, Pauli and his boys would have started shooting. Then all hell would have broken loose."

"You're safe now. That's the only thing that matters. You handled yourself beautifully."

"I just don't know, darling. I just don't know if I can go on like this. I never signed up for something like this."

Chapter 12

By the end of November, the onset of cold weather increased fears of another upswing in Covid-19. Acceptance of the new bivalent vaccine had been weak. When public health and government authorities urged vaccination of toddlers, many adults shook their heads in wonder. This recommendation only stiffened resistance to vaccination. Maskless people were mixing indiscriminately in bars, restaurants, and other public venues. A few public health authorities and schoolteachers made tepid recommendations about a new mask mandate. They were greeted with derision and then ignored.

The war in Ukraine continued to go against the Russian military. They retreated from Kherson City in the south and said they were setting up defensive positions across the Dnipro River. The Ukrainian military announced they intended to liberate the Crimean Peninsula. The Russians responded by sending cruise missiles at power stations and other civilian targets, plunging much of Ukraine into darkness and cold.

Valentin Kostakovich Constantin fled to the British Virgin Islands in his Gulfstream G550, accompanied by his current girlfriend, a small retinue of bodyguards and sycophants, and the diamonds his late brother had brought into the country. He assumed his brother's identity and continued their money laundering operation with the cooperation of Sunshine Investment Bank in Road Town, where his brother had been a large depositor. Dmitry Scull simply disappeared.

In St. Albans, Moselle left a voice message inviting Helen and Frank for Thanksgiving dinner. When they didn't respond, Barney walked up to the house and found Frank sprawled on the sofa, a half-empty bottle of Grappa on the coffee table beside him. "What's up, Frank? How come you didn't respond to our invitation?"

"Helen's disappeared. I can't find her anywhere."

"When did you last see her?"

She walked out of here two days ago … said she was going shopping. She never came back."

"You checked around? I know she likes Neiman's and Saks at the Plaza. That might be the place to start."

"They know her there, and they say they haven't seen her. I called the places where she likes to shop and eat, and they all say the same thing. I think she's left town. After she had been gone a day, I checked around the house. I don't know much about her clothes and shoes, but I saw the XM5 and Sig Rattler were gone. That tells me more than anything she's left town. She only takes her little Sig handgun with her when she shops."

"Where would she go?"

"I think she might go to Omaha … maybe Chicago. I know she doesn't like New York. She had a bad experience with the theaters there."

"I'll get Vinnie to check out Chicago. Tell me where she might be in Omaha, and I'll check that out."

"I don't know much about her life in Omaha."

"Frank, you've got to snap out of it. We need to look for her and fast. The world has become a dangerous place for all of us."

Two days later Barney returned to the blufftop house and found Frank still sprawled on the sofa, another bottle of Grappa beside him. A cable news program showed Margaret Benson speaking in front of the Treasury Department building in Washington. Barney began to report on the futile search for Helen when Frank pointed toward the television.

"We broke up a large international money laundering scheme in New York and Chicago," Margaret said. "We caught them through bank records and surveillance methods that I cannot disclose. The principals are two brothers, Valentin Constantin in New York City and Vladimir Constantin in Moldova. They are both Russian nationals. Unfortunately, their bank in Chisinau in Moldova is still operating. Acting with the Cypriot authorities, we shut down their bank in Limassol. That was their main conduit to the West."

"What about the two brothers?" a reporter asked.

"Unfortunately, they have fled the country. We know at least one of them is in Road Town, in the British Virgin Islands. They're probably both there. We have wire fraud and money laundering charges pending against them, and we intend to extradite them. The extradition treaty with the BVI is a little murky, but we will get them back to face justice one way or another. The important thing is that we shut down their U.S. operation. They'll never do business in this country again. We think they were a conduit for the oligarchs' money to escape our sanctions."

The D.C. press seemed to be in awe of Margaret. They continued to feed her questions that reinforced her narrative … the image of a fearless government corruption fighter.

Frank clicked off the television. "Looks like our Margaret came out of this thing smelling like a rose. I predict she'll go far in government … maybe even become a politician."

"I'm sorry to tell you we can't find Helen. Vinnie has his people scouring Chicago. We came up empty in Omaha. Do you know where else she might have gone?"

"I'm not surprised. When she sets her mind to something, she can be quite formidable. What can you tell me about the other players in what Helen would call our little drama?"

"Frank, I hate to break this to you, but you've been the author, producer, director, and principal actor in what you call this little drama of ours."

"I know. What about the others?"

"Pauli has been demoted to soldier. He screwed up twice. Vito is furious with him because he's afraid of losing the license to Vinnie's warehousing software. I think they've got him working the streets in New Haven or Hartford."

"What about the FBI guy, Peter Andrews?"

"He's put in for early retirement ... he's planning to grow his grapes in Ste. Genevieve in a vineyard he has down there. I've talked to him several times. I kind of like him. I think he wanted the money to go to Ukraine all along."

"What about the three Wagner thugs?"

The FBI and the immigration people picked them up at Kennedy Airport. They were holding passports from the Central African Republic. The Feds had to let them fly to Nairobi since there were no charges pending against them."

"I doubt we've heard the last from them."

"Ukraine wants to put them on trial as war criminals, but the Ukrainian authorities are having trouble getting their legal act together. There's a shooting war going on over there."

Frank clicked on the stereo. Barney poured himself a glass of Grappa and sat in a wingchair across from Frank. After a few minutes, he said, "What's that music, Frank? That's some of the saddest music I've ever heard."

"It's John Corigliano's *First Symphony.*"

"Why is it so sad? That's really depressing stuff. You listen to that long enough, you'll want to overdose on something. Your choice seems to be Grappa."

"He's lamenting all the friends he lost in the AIDS epidemic."

"Look, Frank, this is not good. You've got to pull your-self out of this funk you're in. You're beginning to act like you did when you were at Beaumont during the lock-down. Think, man, where could Helen be? What about the guy you know in Florida? The guy who owns all the lakes down there."

"You're talking about TH. I suppose I could call him. He might know something about her. And nobody owns the lakes. They just own the property around the lakes."

"Do it, man. She could be in danger, and I don't need a seminar on real estate. This is serious."

∾

Three days later, Frank had meandered for hours along the dirt roads circling Lake Hansen near Interlachen, Florida. He finally came upon a remarkably old man in a golf cart, who directed him to the house that TH was building. "Oh, you're talking about Teddy Harper" he said. "That's his house over there on the far side of the lake. He's building it himself, and he's taking his own sweet time about it."

"I recognize the house," Frank said. "I saw it a year ago when he started work on it. But I can't seem to find the road that goes to it."

"You go back to the pavement and follow it until it stops. You'll see two little dirt roads going off to the right. Follow the second one and keep bearing left around the lake. You'll get to his house eventually."

Frank thoroughly explored the two dirt roads for another hour before he saw Helen's white Mercedes 300 sedan parked just off the road. He had missed it the first time he drove through. It was twilight when he stepped out of his car. The partially finished house was set in pine trees and scrub oaks below him. The addition to the structure featured a large front porch overlooking the lake. Frank knew that TH had always done things himself, and the lake house was no exception. Construction debris littered the yard on both sides of the house. He saw a small vineyard farther to one side. A full moon rising in the southeast cast a cobbled path of light straight across the rippled lake to the house. Music wafted up; it was the Platters singing "Magic Touch." He knew Helen had to be inside. She loved the Platters. When he approached the door, the music changed to Puccini's "Un Bel Di" from *Madama Butterfly*. He knocked on the door as Helen opened it.

"Oh, it's you," she said. "What took you so long?"

"You're a very difficult person to find. We looked all over Omaha and Chicago. Then I thought of TH. I called him and asked about you. I had to call him several times. He was reluctant to talk about you. That told me he knew where you were. He said you didn't want to be found before he finally told me where you were. Then he said he thought you missed me."

"He's right about that."

"Look ... my dear ... I don't know how to say this very well. I want you to come home."

Frank tried to kiss her, but Helen pulled back and swelled in righteous anger. "You put me in danger. You put us all in danger. We could have all been killed. And yet you kept at it. Harry in Limassol and Davi in Bangalore. How you concocted such a cockamamie scheme I'll never know. We probably would have all been killed if Rachel hadn't helped you. Her hacking skills always kept you a step ahead of your enemies. I have never been so frightened in my life. I felt like you dragged us down a well of deceit and lies...and all for a cause you had no business being involved in." Helen only stopped when she had to take a breath.

"I know what I did was foolhardy and wrong. I'm asking you to come back. I don't want to live with only my memories. I want to make new memories with you. I promise you I'll try my best to do better."

"Your version of better may not be good enough. I hear you're broke."

"That seems to be general knowledge. I'm surprised it's known all the way down here. The Feds made me pay a big fine and sign a consent order to stay out of banking for ten years. That's a life sentence for me."

"I also hear you've been kicked out of St. Albans."

"Bad news travels fast." Frank paused and considered what to say next. "We've found two small places across the river near Defiance. We're relocating what's left of our operation over there. It's beautiful wine country. I know you'd like it, and I think we can be safe. We've leased our St. Albans compound to a Sicilian family from St. Louis. They're big in the restaurant business in the city. Moselle is about to have her baby. Rachel's won't be far behind her."

"I know all about that too. What you've been doing is all over the internet. They're even putting short clips about what you did on Instagram and TikTok. The financial commentators on cable TV say you're the first person to finance a Ponzi scheme with your own money. You're nearly famous. They'll be calling it a Palermo scheme next."

"I'm asking you to come home. My life's not good without you."

"I'm happy here and I feel safe. I'm difficult to find. You proved that. I sat on the porch and watched what I assumed was you driving around the lake for hours. That was entertaining. I have a quiet life here. Teddy comes over and works on the house most days. I take a chair out to the front lawn and read and enjoy the view while he bangs away. He's living in a big trailer a little ways around the lake. He's also got a warehouse over there with all his stuff inside. He's quite the collector."

"I know you don't like to cook. How are you surviving out here?"

"Frozen microwave dinners go a long way. I'm cooking a little some nights. We go into Palatka occasionally for dinner. They have decent barbeque and seafood. I could almost become a Southerner if they didn't try to fry everything."

"I hope you're not falling for him."

"I knew you'd say that. He's a little eccentric, but he's a perfect gentleman ... unlike some people I know. Where are you staying?"

"I'm at a motel in Palatka. It's on the river. You should see the sunrise over the river. It's beautiful."

"You could stay here."

"I just want you to come home."

"I'll have to think about it. I think you just want some of your money back from my trust fund now that you're broke."

"The money I put in your trust fund is yours and always will be. I'm essentially working for Barney and Moselle now. He followed my investment strategies and did well over the last few years. And he didn't give away any of his profits. The Cypriot prosecutors are saying they want to put me in jail. That means I can't travel to any EU country. They've effectively shut down Suyu Bank. Harry Gallanis got out of Cyprus just in time. Barney's lawyers are trying to work out a deal with them."

"Good for Barney. I'm happy one person in our group has some financial and legal sense. I'm sure you'll find ways to make money again. That's one thing you know how to do."

"Like I told you, the SEC has banished me from the U.S. banking system and restricted my brokerage activities for the next ten years. That essentially closes me out permanently."

"I'm sure you deserved it. You're lucky the Feds didn't put you in jail. That Margaret Benson likes to take scalps."

"Please come home. I'll get down on my knees and beg you if that's what you want."

I told you I'll have to think about it. The one thing I know right now is I want you to stay here with me tonight. I'm lonely. It's too quiet here. I like the noise you make."

The End

About the Author

Thomas Morgan is Thomas Morgan Hyers, a practicing pulmonologist in St. Louis. He is in the same age group as the two principal characters in the *Helen and Frank* stories, and he continues to experience the pandemic years of Covid-19 in his medical practice and in his personal interactions with family and friends. This is his third book in the series, in which he weaves the effect of the pandemic on the lives of his fictional characters. He practices pulmonary occupational medicine and conducts clinical research with new pharmaceuticals. In addition to his medical responsibilities and writing efforts, he likes to spend time with his family, garden and cook.

www.ingramcontent.com/pod-product-compliance
Lightning Source LLC
Chambersburg PA
CBHW070358200726

48294CB00003B/979